PENGUIN BOOKS

SOMETHING NASTY IN THE WOODSHED

Kyril Bonfiglioli was born in Eastbourne in 1928 of an English mother and Italo-Slovene father, and after studying at Oxford University and spending five years in the army, took up a career as an art dealer, the same career as his eccentric creation, Charlie Mortdecai. He lived in Ireland and then in Jersey, where he died in 1985. Penguin publish all three Mortdecai novels (*Don't Point That Thing at Me*, *After You with the Pistol* and *Something Nasty in the Woodshed*) as well as *All the Tea in China*, a historical novel featuring a disreputable ancestor of Mortdecai and *The Great Mortdecai Moustache Mystery*, which was left unfinished at his death and was completed by Craig Brown.

An accomplished fencer, a fair shot with most weapons and a serial marrier of beautiful women, Bonfiglioli claimed to be 'abstemious in all things except drink, food, tobacco and talking' and 'loved and respected by all who knew him slightly'.

Something Nasty in
the Woodshed

KYRIL BONFIGLIOLI

PENGUIN BOOKS

PENGUIN BOOKS

Published by the Penguin Group
Penguin Books Ltd, 80 Strand, London WC2R 0RL, England
Penguin Group (USA) Inc., 375 Hudson Street, New York, New York 10014, USA
Penguin Group (Canada), 90 Eglinton Avenue East, Suite 700, Toronto, Ontario, Canada M4P 2Y3
(a division of Pearson Penguin Canada Inc.)
Penguin Ireland, 25 St Stephen's Green, Dublin 2, Ireland (a division of Penguin Books Ltd)
Penguin Group (Australia), 707 Collins Street, Melbourne, Victoria 3008, Australia
(a division of Pearson Australia Group Pty Ltd)
Penguin Books India Pvt Ltd, 11 Community Centre, Panchsheel Park, New Delhi – 110 017, India
Penguin Group (NZ), 67 Apollo Drive, Rosedale, Auckland 0632, New Zealand
(a division of Pearson New Zealand Ltd)
Penguin Books (South Africa) (Pty) Ltd, Block D, Rosebank Office Park,
181 Jan Smuts Avenue, Parktown North, Gauteng 2193, South Africa

Penguin Books Ltd, Registered Offices: 80 Strand, London WC2R 0RL, England

www.penguin.com

First published by Macmillan London Ltd 1976
First published by Penguin Books in *The Mortdecai Trilogy* 2001
Reissued in this edition 2014
003

Copyright © the Estate of Kyril Bonfiglioli, 1976
All rights reserved

The moral right of the copyright holders has been asserted

Printed in Great Britain by Clays Ltd, St Ives plc

ISBN: 978-0-241-97027-0

4/15   5600 5126

www.greenpenguin.co.uk

Et Amicorum

Because I do not expect to survive to write another novel about Jersey, I must ask, in alphabetical order, Alan, Angela, Barry, Betty, Bobbie, Dick, Gordon, Heather, Hugh, Jean, Joan, John, Mary, Nick, Olive, Paul, Peter, Rosemary, Stanley, Terry, Topper, Vera – and a hundred other kindly Jersey folk to accept this as a trifling repayment for all their kindness and tolerance. I hope, too, that they will not mind if I add the names of a black Labrador named Pompey and a canary called Bert.

The epigraphs are all by Swinburne, except one which is a palpable forgery.

None of the people in this novel bears any intentional resemblance to any real person: real people are far too improbable for use in fiction.

The Honorary Police of Jersey are used to being teased: all those whom I have had the pleasure of meeting are just, honourable, intelligent and can take a joke.

I must not thank by name all the kindly Jersey folk who have answered my countless questions – that would be a poor recompense for their patience.

The fictional narrator is a nasty, waspish man: pray do not confuse him with the author, who is gentle and kind.

The Swinburne forgery is, in a way, signed.

I

Till the slow sea rise and the sheer cliff crumble,
Till terrace and meadow the deep gulfs drink,
Till the strength of the waves of the high tides humble
The fields that lessen, the rocks that shrink,
Here now in his triumph where all things falter,
Stretched out on the spoils that his own hand spread,
As a god self-slain on his own strange altar,
Death lies dead.

A Forsaken Garden

The Islands

Seven thousand years ago – give or take a few months – a great deal of water left the North Sea for good reasons of its own which I cannot recall off-hand and poured over the lower parts of North-West Europe, forming the English Channel and effectively separating England from France, to the mutual gratification of both parties (for if it had not happened, you see, we English would have been foreigners and the French would have had to eat bread sauce).

Not much later the sea scoured away at some of the craggier bits of the French coast and separated part of the higher ground from the mainland. You call the resulting islands the Channel Isles because you know no better: their true and ancient name is *Les Iles Normandes*. It has been argued that they do not belong to the

United Kingdom but rather the other way about, for they were part of the Duchy of Normandy long before William did his conquering in England – and they are the only surviving parts of that Duchy. They are fiercely loyal to the Crown and the toast is still 'The Queen – our Duke'. The Isles all have different, ancient and peculiar laws and constitutions, as well as some pretty odd customs. Of which more later.

This Island

It is called Jersey and is constructed of granite, shale, diorite and porphyrite, as every schoolboy knows. The whole thing is sort of tilted so that it faces south, which I'm sure is good for the weather. (I never discuss the weather; that is for resort-owners, the peasantry, and certain gentle maniacs who choose to inhabit the Admiralty roof.) The coastline is wild and lovely past belief.

Tobacco and ardent spirits are cheap and income tax benignly low but I dare say these blessings will vanish, along with the Public Schools, as soon as the Socialists get a real majority and start to feel their oats.

The People

There are many layers of these. First, the holiday-makers, who need no description, bless them. Their name is legion.

Next, the farmers, who are all of old Jersiais stock, and, in an unobtrusive and po-faced way, run the Island to their own quiet satisfaction. They have ugly old names, ugly old faces and *hideous* old wives. Their workers are like them but drunker. Some transient peasants drift in from Normandy, Brittany and even Wales to see to the daffodil, potato and tomato harvests; they are small and squat and sinister, like Italians from the Abruzzi, and they are the drunkest of all and who shall blame them.

Third, and best known, are the rich immigrants who have come to enjoy the Isle's peculiar tax benefits. The modest tax they pay swells the local coffers in a way the Jerseyman finds hard to forgive. Some of them are total abstainers, which I suppose is one way of becoming rich, but most of them are pretty drunk too: whisky is about the same price as cheap wine – and much nicer.

They have brought so much money with them that I sometimes

fear the Isle may one day sink beneath its weight. Their conversation is brilliant so long as you stick to the subject of the length of their drawing-rooms – or 'lounges' as they are called in the local *argot*.

Hordes of bankers and other money-borrowers, of every degree of venality, have followed them here like greedy shite-hawks and each prime site in St Helier is snapped up by these shameless guzzlers as soon as it falls vacant. This is probably a bad thing.

There are several minor categories like nobility and gentry, Portuguese waiters, Indian trumpery-mongers, transient barmaids and drunken novelists but these, although uniformly nice, concern our story but little.

The Fauna

The prop of the economy, and the only large mammal other than the Jersey lady, is the Jersey cow. She is doe-eyed and quite beautiful and secretes wonderfully rich milk. She is usually tethered because pasture is precious and fences are costly; in winter she is 'rugged' with a plastic mackintosh and in summer she sports a sun-bonnet. Yes, truly. There are some pigs but I believe no sheep, which is perhaps why a certain Highland Regiment has never been stationed here. There is a great number of horses and the suburban cavalry may be seen tittuping along the lanes at any hour of the day.

Wild-life is scarce except for sea-birds; the dominant species are the magpie and the sparrow. There is no shooting land and therefore no gamekeepers, so the ubiquitous magpie munches up all the nestlings; only the sparrow, that bird of Venus, can outbreed magpies by diddling his mate all the year round, sturdy little chap. In the late autumn small rare birds may sometimes be seen on passage, resting in the fields of unborn daffodils.

The Flora

This is chiefly grass and gardening, the latter often of an excruciating garishness. There is some bracken and gorse on parcels of land waiting for planning permission but all the rest is luxury crops: early potatoes, daffodils, anemones, tomatoes and the occasional shy cauliflower. Certain cabbages with prodigally long stalks are grown for tourists to photograph: the natives assure them with straight faces that these are grown for walking-sticks but no one in his senses would believe that, would he?

The Buildings

These range from the gloomy to the absurd via the pretentious. St Helier is a positive barrel of architectural fun: even Sir John Betjeman would be unable to keep a straight face. In the countryside the characteristic building is a large, grim farmhouse made of liver-coloured granite, with huge outer walls and a shortage of windows. Rich incomers grab them avidly and modernize them hideously. The finished article is worth ten times the price of a comparable house in England. I don't know whether that's a good thing or not.

The Language

This is rather a difficult bit. Your actual Jerseyman of the artisan classes speaks something which sounds quite like English until you try to understand it, then you realize that it is like an Australian trying to imitate a Liverpudlian. 'His' is pronounced 'ease' and most sentences begin with the phrase 'My Chri' and end with the vocable 'eh?' It is an unlovely tongue and one can readily learn to dislike it.

Laws and other official matter are written in a quaint old Norman-French reminiscent of Domesday-Book Latin. Members of the grand old Jersey families can still speak it, I'm told, but you won't get them to admit it.

The true *patois Jersiais* is something quite different and barbarous beyond belief. (*Guinness es bouan por té*.) When I tell you that the word 'Jersey' represents the Latin 'Caesarea' I think you will take my meaning.

Finally, most tradespeople can produce enough schoolboy French of modern vintage to puzzle the transient workers with, especially since the latter are usually tired and drunk.

The Police

There is a small body of men, based in St Helier, called the Paid Police. I'm sure they love that. They are much like English police but fewer and not so angry. They have uniforms and equipment; they seem honest and amiable; they don't hit people. Unlike some I could name.

Much more important (outside St Helier) are the Honorary Police, who are of course unpaid. They do not wear uniforms – you are supposed to *know* who they are. Each of the twelve Parishes has a Connétable; under him are the Centeniers, each of whom in theory, protects and disciplines a hundred families and leads five Vingteniers who guard twenty families each. These are all elective posts but elections rarely afford any surprises, if you see what I mean, and in any case there is little competition for these honours.

No one is legally under arrest in Jersey until a Centenier has tapped him on the shoulder with his absurd, tiny truncheon of office (you can imagine how the Paid Police like *that* rule) and it is said that a Centenier who has mislaid his truncheon wrenches off the handle from the nearest lavatory chain. Luckily, Centeniers do not often feel it necessary to arrest their friends, neighbours and cousins, unless the offence is grave, and thus a great deal of public money is saved and a great many lavatories are left intact. It works quite well, really. The Centenier takes his erring neighbour for a quiet chat and puts the fear of God in him, thus preventing a recurrence of the offence much more effectively than an expensive trial, a suspended sentence and a year of reporting to some mud-brained Probation Officer with a diploma in Social Science from Nersdley Polytechnic.

One of the Houses

It belongs to Sam Davenant and is called La Gouluterie, from a water-meadow which is part of the estate. This probably takes its name from Simon le Goulue who was Connétable of S. Magloire Parish in 1540, but zealous antiquaries suspect that *goulues* – round-bellied pottery crocks for seething beans in – were once potted in this clayey field. I suspect that Simon or one of his forebears was called 'le Goulue' because he was a bit of a bean-crock himself.

5

The dottier kind of amateur antiquary will, of course, assure you that the name has something to do with fertility-rites, but then they always do, don't they?

Much of the building dates from the sixteenth century and there are traces of earlier work and hints of religious use. It is of a pleasant, pink granite of the sort no longer quarried and it has been tactfully coaxed into a state of comfort and dignity. There are tourelles, rondelines, bénitiers and so forth – I'm sure you know what all those are. For my part, I forget. Most of the front is at the back – doors, terraces and so on – but the front proper faces a sunny, agreeable courtyard on the other side of which lies the Other House, which belongs to Sam's best friend.

The Other House

This belongs to George Breakspear who is Sam's best friend and it is called Les Cherche-fuites – I don't know what that means. It has been extensively dandified in the eighteenth century and its windows, because of the exigencies of the underlying granite, are all slightly out of kilter, which rescues it from the drab symmetry of most houses of that period. Like La Gouluterie, much of its front is at the back (gardens, pool etc.) and at the back, too, there is a curious and engaging porch with concave glazing of the kind associated in Jersey with 'cod houses' – places built in the piping times of the cod industry when dozens of daring Jersey skippers ventured to the Grand Banks and suddenly found themselves rich. At one side there is an ugly Victorian stable of yellow brick with a clock which doesn't go.

Consider, Then,

These two agreeable houses beaming affably at each other across the old stone cider-press in the centre of the courtyard; consider, too, how rare and fortunate it is that the owners should be such firm friends. (The fact that the owners' wives loathe each other's essential tripes is of little importance, one supposes, and indeed it rarely comes to the surface even when they are alone.)

Consider, Too

The proprietors of these houses, starting with George Breakspear of Les Cherche-fuites. George believes in God, but only the C. of E. brand, as advertised on television by virtue of the Equal Time Agreement, although he has an Open Mind because he has seen some Pretty Queer Things in India and places like that. His manners are too good to let his religion show, which is as it should be. He is not a fool. You would guess that he had been a brevet major in the War; in fact he was a full and substantive brigadier and holds the DSO, the MC and many another bauble but, here again, his too stringent manners forbid him to use either the rank or the ribandry in civil life. (This is going a little too far, I think: it is subtly *rude* to keep your honours in your handkerchief drawer along with the french letters. Give me, any day, those jolly European hussar officers who swagger out at night in their splendid comic-opera uniforms, rather than those po-faced English Guardees who change, at the drop of a bowler hat, into sad imitations of solvent stockbrokers. Officers should have dash and debts and drabs and, above all, duns, whom they can horsewhip outside their quarters to give them an appetite for breakfast, don't you agree?)

George is of middle height, average appearance and normal weight. His friends do not always recognize him, which is what it's all about, isn't it. In his favourite armchair in his club they recognize him, of course, because he's *there* you see. The better sort of bartenders recognize him, too, but that's their job.

His clothes are in such quiet good taste that they almost amount to a disguise, a cloak of invisibility, perhaps.

Despite this greyish coloration one somehow knows for certain that, were the Hun or Boche to invade us, George would not only spring capably to arms on the instant but would, without debate or question, assume command by invoking some ancient English password, token or shibboleth which we would all recognize, although hearing it for the first time since King Arthur sank below the waves of that lake near Avalon.

In the meantime, however, here and now in Jersey, one certainly didn't want not to know him, for he listened to one's stories; he poured big (but not vulgarly big) drinks; did not smile too unhappily if one swore in front of his wife and, if the party lasted too long for him, he didn't make going-to-bed noises, he just sort of faded away and re-materialized, one supposes, in his dressing-room.

He drinks quite a lot in a diffident sort of way; there's no shooting in Jersey, you see, and that makes the winter days rather long unless you happen to be over-sexed.

He scraped a sort of degree at Cambridge and won a boxing blue – one almost says 'of course' – and he is knowledgeable about the Napoleonic wars. He is one of those enviable people who – like Balliol men – are serenely certain that what they do and think and are is right. This inability to see any flaws in oneself is a branch of pottiness, of course, but much less harmful than being unable to see any good in oneself.

George cannot quite understand why we gave up India and he is a little puzzled about Suez. He polishes his shoes himself; they are all old, crackled and expensive.

He is, or was, what used to be called a gentleman, or have I said that already?

George's Wife

is called Sonia, although her women-friends say that the name on her birth-certificate was probably Ruby. It is hard to say why she and George married; you sometimes catch them stealing puzzled glances at each other as though they, too, were wondering still.

She is a slut and a bitch, every woman can tell this at a glance, so can most homosexuals. Nice young men can persuade themselves that her languishing glances are for them alone, although they should surely be able to see that her instructions to the gardener about bedding-out are an equally clear invitation to bedding-in. George believes in her, I think, but like Matilda's aunt, the effort sometimes nearly kills him. She is flashy by nature, choice and art: her eyes are deep blue and enormous, her skin is like magnolia petals and her hair is so black that it seems to be Navy-blue. Her breasts, when they are lugged up and squashed together by her valuable brassière, resemble nothing so much as the bum of a beautiful child, but when she is naked they are lax and unpleasing, the muscle tone long gone. I happen to prefer a breast that I can hold in one hand, don't you? – but I know that Americans, for instance, prefer quantity, if you'll forgive the pun.

Under a shellac-layer of cultivation and coffee-table books her manners and morals are those of a skilled whore who has succeeded in retiring early and now dedicates her craft to personal pleasure alone. She is very good at it indeed. I dare say.

While by no means mutton-dressed-as-lamb she is nevertheless subtly wrongly clothed, in that and in one other respect. She wears clothes exactly three years too young for her – never more, never less – and, like those men who contrive always to have two days' growth of beard – never more, never less – just so she is always expensively dressed in the height of last year's fashion: never quite up-to-date nor ever quite out of it.

This of course pleases her women friends mightily, although their menfolk do not twig and are in any case more concerned with admiring Sonia's teats.

She is, of course, an accomplished liar but then they all are, aren't they? (Or aren't you married?) George is quite clever enough to detect her in her falsehoods but both breeding and common-sense forbid this in him.

Sonia and George have two sons. One of them, very clever, is serving out the last of his stretch at a school called Wellington; Sonia does not mind having a son at school – although she manages to give the impression that he is at *prep* school – but she is a little cross at the existence of the other son who is what is called grown-up. He is marvellously stupid and drives a helicopter for the Army or Navy or some such out-dated nonsense. He is always breaking their valuable aircraft but his superiors never seem to mind, they just buy him a new one. They don't pay for it themselves, you see. You do.

Now Sam Davenant

and straight away we detect a falsehood, an affectation, for no one has been christened Sam for a hundred years. His real name is Sacheverell, of course. At school he would have died rather than divulge this but nowadays he quite likes one to find out.

He affects to be affected, which he is otherwise not, if you see what I mean, and hopes that his chief fault, congenital idleness or *accidie*, will pass as an affectation. His infrequent swings to the manic phase, made much of, help him to carry this off.

He would think shame to be seen out of bed before noon – unless he had been up all night – and has eaten no breakfast for twenty years.

He is almost tiresomely well-read. In public he is usually immersed in a trashy paper-back but it is quite certain that in his bedroom he reads Gibbon, Fénelon, Horace and 'tous ces defunts cockolores'. On the other hand, he stoutly denies that he has ever heard of Marcuse and Borges, whoever they may be. (For my part, I adamantly believe in teaching Fénelon, Racine, Milton and Gibbon to the young as soon as may be; you cannot learn too early in life that most classical literature is both dull and unimportant.)

Sam is absurdly kind, easy-going, tolerant and has a harsh word for no one, but I have long recognized in him an insane iron core which would make him, if ultimately provoked, a very bad enemy indeed. He used to play backgammon uncommonly well until the sparks took it up, whereupon he dropped it; he's like that. I can sometimes beat him at poker.

He seems to be quite rich in a vague sort of way but no one knows how or whence. He hints naughtily at gun-running or worse in his youth – perhaps white-slaving – but I suspect a string of dry-cleaning shops in Northern Ireland: why else should he be so vexed about the news of bomb-outrages in Belfast?

He is tall, pale, curly-haired, thickening a little and a trifle older than me. Let us say fifty.

On the Other Hand

his wife is tiny, sweet, silly and called Violet, if you'll believe it. Sam calls her The Shrinker. She does, indeed, shrink from most things; I've watched her often. Sam treats her with amused tolerance but secretly adores her, if I may quote from the women's weeklies. She is nervously vulnerable and can blush and even faint, just as they used to in the olden days.

On rare occasions she is an inspired cook but most of the time she burns or otherwise ruins food but, luckily, Sam is not greedy and can cook. I must not pretend to any knowledge of their nuptial relationships but I should think on the whole probably not. He treats her with a courtesy so elaborate that you might be forgiven for thinking that he hated her, but you would be wrong.

There is something vaguely mysterious about Violet's mother who is always referred to as 'poor mummy'. She is, I suppose, either potty or an alcoholic or kleptomaniac or some such nonsense and there are times when I wonder a little about Violet herself: her verbal habits are odd and she tends to say things like 'rabbits breed like hot cakes'.

And Now, For My Last Trick

this is the narrator, or, if you'll pardon the accidence, me. My name is Charlie Mortdecai (I was actually *christened* Charlie: I think my mother was subtly getting at my father) and I'm a Honble because my father used to be – and my brother (God rot his soul) is – a Baron, which is a kind of failed Viscount, you might say, if you cared about that sort of nonsense. As my father did.

For the time being I live just a few furlongs across the fields from the two houses in half of a lovely mansion (a mansion, according to estate agents and other housemongers, is a house with two staircases) called Wutherings with my absurdly beautiful new Austrian-Jewish-American wife, Johanna, and my equally unbelievable one-eyed, one-fanged thug, Jock. (I'm by way of being an art-dealer, you see, which is why I have to keep a thug.) I'm not here permanently; I haven't enough money to make it worth while dodging taxes and my wife has too much of it to bother. I really live in London but, although I'm not exactly *persona non grata* there, a particular branch of the police sort of prefers me to live outside the place for a while. You wouldn't be interested in the reason and there's nothing in the fine print that says I can't be a little shady, is there?

Nor would you be interested in my reasons for having married Johanna, suffice it to say that it was not for her money. She loves me fiercely, for reasons which are a mystery to me, and I have come to like her very much. We don't understand each other in the least, which is probably a good thing, but we agree fervently that Mozart is marvellous and Wagner vulgar. She doesn't care to talk very much, which is the prime ingredient for a happy marriage: in Runyon's deathless words – 'Naturally, a doll who is willing to listen instead of wishing to gab herself is bound to be popular because if there is anything most citizens hate and despise it is a gabby doll.'

In any case, we are, in an important sense, worlds apart for she is devoted to the game of Contract Bridge – a kind of lunatic whist – whilst I dearly love Gin Rummy which Johanna loathes because it is too utterly simple-minded and perhaps because I always win. She really is quite astonishingly beautiful* but too well-bred to flutter her eyelashes at other men. We never quarrel; the nearest we ever got to it was once, when I was being intolerable: she quietly said, 'Charlie dear, which of us shall leave the room?'

All three of our houses stand in the parish of S. Magloire, the smallest parish in Jersey. It is wedged between S. Jean and Trinity and has a short coastline of its own at Belle Etoile Bay – just East – or is it West? – of Bonne Nuit Bay. Such pretty names, I always think.

* See *Don't Point That Thing at Me.*

2

And Pan by noon and Bacchus by night,
Fleeter of foot than the fleet-foot kid,
Follows with dancing and fills with delight
The Mænad and the Bassarid;
And soft as lips that laugh and hide
The laughing leaves of the trees divide,
And screen from seeing and leave in sight
The god pursuing, the maiden hid.

Atalanta in Calydon

It all started – or at any rate the narrative I have to offer all started – at Easter last year: that season when we remind each other of the judicial murder of a Jewish revolutionary two thousand years ago by distributing chocolate eggs to the children of people we dislike.

I had been in a vile temper all day and had cursed Jock roundly. He knew very well that it was only because there had been no newspapers and hence no *Times* crossword, but for reasons of his own he had chosen to sulk. When I asked what was for dinner he pointed out smugly that gentlemen's menservants always have the day off on Easter Monday and, indeed, those with thoughtful masters were often given the whole week-end.

I explained to him kindly that he was not a proper manservant, trained to gentlemen's service, but only a mere thug and that I had noticed lately that he was getting notions above his station in life.

His answer was in the plural – and they bounce.

Shaking with rage at having nursed such a viper in my bosom, I huddled on some clothes and drove off to get dinner in St Helier, my tyres cutting up the gravel savagely and spraying it on to the lawn. (The gardener had, in any case, been making grumbling noises for weeks and I would be well shot of him: his snail-like working pace had earned him the sobriquet 'Flash' from Johanna.)

In St Helier, the restaurant I had readied my gastric juices for was, of course, closed. It wasn't just Easter Bunny time, it was That Kind of Day, too. That did it. Stomach churning with chagrin and thwarted peptins, I went to the Club, determined to spite myself with cold steak-and-kidney pie and spurious new potatoes forced into pallid maturity in Cyprus with doses of chicken-crut and peasants' pee.

On the steps I met George, coming down.

'Eaten already?' I asked.

'No. Looked at the menu. A shop-girl would eat any quantity of it. I'm off. Come back with me and play backgammon. There's half a duck in the fridge if the maid hasn't swiped it. And you could make one of your potato salads. And I'd open a bottle of that Fleurie you like so much.'

It was a deal. Off we sped, he in his Rover, I in my absurd Mini GT which I bought because I can never resist a contradiction in terms.

As we swung into the courtyard and George killed the engine I heard the screams. He didn't hear them until he'd opened the door of his better-insulated car, so I was first at the door, which was locked. He stabbed it with his key and was through the hall and up the stairs before I had recovered from the mighty shove he had given me.

In the bedroom was his wife, quite bare, legs spread wide and shrieking as though she were approaching a grade on the Atcheson, Topeka and Santa Fé Railroad, Inc.

I couldn't help noticing that her bush, contrary to the usual practice, was of a lighter shade than the hair of her head. The window was open wide and a warm wind stirred the curtains but the room was fragrant with sex. George was already out of the window and taking a grip of the creeper on the wall outside. It ripped loose under his weight and he landed on the gravel below

14

with what I suppose I may as well call a sickening thud and an oath more suitable to the Sergeants' Mess than to his own station in life.

Sonia left off shrieking, pulled a rumpled sheet over her rumpled charms and started concentrating on tragic expressions and ugly gulping noises. I studied her curiously. It was an act, but then she was a woman, so she wasn't necessarily acting, if you follow me. I had never before observed the behaviour-pattern of a recent rape-victim (I can't say *rapée*, can I – it reminds one of that delicious Rapée Morvandelle that one puts into *quiches*.) (It's also a kind of snuff, isn't it?) nor had I any preconceptions as to how such a victim would react, but somehow I found the performance unsatisfying; suspension of disbelief wouldn't quite come. However, there was no time to waste. I had no intention, I need scarcely say, of following George and the rapist out of the window: I am a little portly just at present and I was wearing a new and costly mohair suit, but I felt that something should be done and I felt, too, a little *de trop* in that bedroom.

'There, there,' I said, patting what I took to be her shoulder under the sheet but which proved, embarrassingly, to be what pornographers call a *quivering mound* and she began to steam-whistle again.

'Oops, sorry,' I mumbled as I fled, my carefully-built reputation for being *uno di quelli* shattered.

Downstairs and out through the back door, there was nothing to be seen but the ambiguous outlines of costly shrubs, no smell but the drowsy odours of night-scented whatever-they-ares and no sound but the growling of my still unfilled belly.

George might be anywhere, the rapist still more so, if his exploits had left him with any strength.

'Chemise de femme,
Armure ad hoc
Pour la gaie prise
Et la belle choque'

was running through my head. Sonia's nightdress, the short sort, calculated for sea-level, had been on the floor, you see, suggesting a leisurely and fastidious rapist.

There was nothing to be done out there in the garden; dirty fighting is one of my favourite outdoor sports, believe it or not, but

I do like a little advantage – umbrageous shrubberies bulging with mad rapists are not my notion of advantageous ground. I attribute my long life and good health to cowardice.

I went indoors and lifted the telephone. Then I put it down again. Sonia might not *want* a doctor; probably a bidet and a codeine tablet would fill the bill, if I may coin a phrase. George might not *want* the police or any other third party to learn of the invasion of his wife's secret garden.

What I did was, I made a stiff drink of gin and orange juice and tonic, such as I knew Sonia loved, and carried it up to the bedroom, administering it with many a 'there, there, child'. Then I went downstairs and made a similar confection for myself, except that it was made of whisky and soda. Then I had another which tasted even better and gave me enough lightning-like decision to go across the courtyard and find Sam.

'Sam,' I said, when he answered my knock, 'there is trouble across the way.'

'Only trouble?' he said. 'It sounded like a steam traction-engine rally. I nearly went over but I thought it impertinent to interfere in what might be a private argument.'

I outlined the situation to him and he went to fetch Violet from the other end of the house. Her face was red and tear-stained and I cocked an inquiring eyebrow,

'It's all right,' she said, 'it's just the crabs.'

'The *crabs*?' I cried, shocked by such candour. 'My dear, however did you catch *them*?'

'I didn't. The plumber did.'

'You are weeping because the plumber has contracted crabs?'

Sam would ordinarily have let this go on, relishing Violet's tangled thought-patterns, but time pressed.

'The plumber,' he explained, 'is a keen sea-fisher, as they all are here. He has today given us two fine shanker crabs, alive alive-oh. Violet is boiling them and the sound of their knocking on the saucepan-lid fills her with compassion. *Hinc illae lachry-mae.*'

Violet smiled sweetly, vacantly, through her tears.

A minute later we were at Les Cherche-fuites, where all was going as merrily as a wedding-bell. George was covered with mud, bits of wistaria and gravel-rash, and was making grating, brigadier-like noises into the telephone. Sonia was striking well-raped attitudes reminiscent of Emma Hamilton portraying Lucrece, and was fetching huge and unbecoming sobs up from deep in her thorax. Violet rushed to her and went into the 'there, there' and 'now, now' routine but to no avail, for Sonia merely shifted into the higher register. Violet steered her firmly off to the bathroom to wash her face or whatever women do for each other in times of stress.

George subsided into an armchair, glaring at the tumbler of Scotch I had pressed into his hand.

'Bloody swine,' he growled. 'Raped my wife. Ruined my wistaria.'

'I'll send my man round first thing in the morning to have a look at it,' said Sam. 'The wistaria I mean. They're very tenacious things – soon recover. Wistaria,' he added; gratuitously, it seemed to me.

I started to tiptoe out: I love dramas but I am no sort of horticulturalist.

'Don't go,' said George.

'No, don't go,' said Sam.

I didn't go, I hadn't really wanted to. I wondered whether George had forgotten about the half of a cold duck and bottle of Fleurie. I helped myself to a little more of his Scotch.

'Who were you telephoning, George?' asked Sam.

'Doctor.'

'Wise, d'you think? Bit shaming for Sonia?'

'Irrelevant. Bastard may have damaged her insides, given her some filthy disease, even a brat . . . God knows . . .' His voice trailed off into a choking, hate-filled silence.

'What I have to decide,' he went on quietly, 'is police or not.'

That was, indeed, a matter for thought. Even the Paid Police, if they could eventually be coaxed out from St Helier, could hardly be expected to make much of a possible footprint or two and a ravished wife's incoherent babblings, while the Honorary Police, in the person of the local Vingtenier, pillar of the community though he might be, could do little more than search his brain for known or likely rapists in his twenty families (excluding those to whom he was related, which would rule out most) and then summon his Centenier. The Centenier, excellent and astute man, could do little more than search *his* brain: his appointment and specialized training were approximately those of the Chairman of a Parish Council in England and he had neither the equipment, the men, nor the

17

skills necessary to carry out a drag-net operation or house-to-house search. And what to look for in such a search? Someone breathing hard? Worst of all, such a public fuss would stamp Sonia for ever as the 'poor lady what got raped last Easter'.

'On the whole,' said Sam gently, 'I'd think not.'

'Yes,' I said with my customary ambiguity.

'I see all that,' said George, 'and obviously I agree with it. But there is a citizen's duty. Personal embarrassment shouldn't count. It's the law, d'you see. Much more important than us. Even if it is an ass. Otherwise where are we?'

'But if we know it can't help?' (Sam)

'Well, yes, that's the point, isn't it?' He thought for a while, ignoring the drink in his hand.

'Yes, got it,' he said at length, 'I hold the Queen's commission and in any case there's that citizen's arrest law, isn't there. I'll have a private chat with the Centenier tomorrow, explain my position. Then we three form a *posse comitatus*; hound the swine down. Yes, that's it. Good night, you men. Report here at noon tomorrow. Bring your own sandwiches.'

Sam gazed at him aghast: Nature had not formed him to be a posse-member.

I, too, gazed at him aghast: there was clearly not going to be any cold duck that night.

Violet entered, weeping freely again.

'It is really quite dreadful,' she said, 'poor dear girl. He did *very* odd things to her as well as, well, you know, and she is frightened out of her wits. He must have been a maniac, he was wearing a mask and funny-smelling clothes, and, oh yes, he had a sword painted on his tummy.'

George growled and cursed a bit; Sam's eyebrows shot up and I began to muse furiously.

'Bloody bastard,' said George.

'How perfectly extraordinary,' said Sam.

'What kind of a mask?' I asked.

The others looked at me, a touch of rebuke in their eyes, as though I had said 'District Nurse' in front of the children.

'One of those joke-shop rubber masks, she thinks. You know, Dracula or the Beast from 5,000 Fathoms.'

'Just so,' I said. 'The Beast.'

'Aha! said Sam. 'I think I twig. But the sword thing is new, isn't it?'

'Yes, but I think it fits.'

'How?'

'Not sure enough now, tell you some other time.'

'Would somebody mind telling *me*,' snarled George, 'what the f—' he paused, collected himself. 'Sorry,' he resumed, 'I mean, I don't quite follow you men.'

'The Beast of Jersey,' Sam explained. 'You know, the chap who terrorized the Island for a dozen years; used to creep into children's rooms, carry them out of the window, do odd things to them in the fields – not always very nasty – then pop them back into their little beds. The police think that there may have been more than a hundred such assaults but naturally most of them were not reported, for reasons which you will, um, appreciate. He used to wear a rubber mask, most of the victims said that he had an odd smell and he wore bizarre clothes, studded with nails. Just before you moved here they caught a chap called Paisnel, who is now serving thirty years, rightly or wrongly.'

'Shouldn't like to be him,' I interjected, 'convicts are madly sentimental and they do *beastly* things to offenders against children. Make them sing alto, see what I mean.'

'Yes. I dare say they do. No experience in that field myself. Take your word for it.'

That was cheaper than Sam's usual level of badinage; I made a mental note to see that he suffered for it. I'm not a vengeful chap but I can't allow my friends to make cheap witticisms, can I? It's a question of the quality of life.

'What was interesting,' Sam went on as I chewed my spleen, 'was that Paisnel kept on saying that it was "all part of something" but he wouldn't say what and he said that when he was arrested he was on his way to meet "certain people" but he wouldn't say whom.'

'Perfectly obvious,' said George; 'the beggar was one of these witches or witchmasters. It all comes back to me now. The plumber told me all about it when he came in drunk just after Christmas. Seems it wasn't this Paisnel fellow at all, all the locals know who it was, including most of the Honorary Police . . . or did he say that Paisnel was just part of it?'

'That strain again,' murmured Sam, 'it hath a dying fall . . .'

'Quite right. And this Paisnel had a secret room, hadn't he, with a pottery frog or toad in it and *that* was supposed to be "part of it" too. And there was one of these Papist Palm Sunday crosses in the car he was nabbed in and they say he screamed when they asked him to touch it.'

'Codswallop?' I prompted.

'Not necessarily. Seen too many funny things myself to be ready to scoff at, ah, funny things.'

'In India, I dare say?'

He glared at me suspiciously.

'Yes,' curtly. 'There and elsewhere. Well, mustn't keep you chaps any longer. Good of you to help, very.'

Hunger stabbed me as I drove home. There was nothing inviting in the fridge, certainly not the half of a cold duck, but I happen to know where Jock hides his 'perks' and I spitefully wolfed a whole tin of caviare (the real Grosrybrest; Jock steals nothing but the best, he spurns Beluga and Ocietrova) on hot toast and left the kitchen in a horrid mess. On purpose.

Upstairs, Johanna appeared to be asleep and I slunk gratefully into bed like a thief in the night.

'Gotcha!' she yelled triumphantly.

'Have a care, for God's sake, you'll have me singing alto.'

'Where have you been, you naughty little stud?'

I told her the whole story and she listened enthralled.

'Let's play rapists,' she said when I had finished.

'I'm not climbing through any bloody window.'

'I'll let you off that bit.'

'But I haven't a rubber mask.'

'*Extemporize.*'

'Oh, really.'

'I shall pretend to be asleep and you shall *sneak* into the room and *leap* upon me and work your wicked will and I shall scream and scream but very softly so as not to wake our nice landlord.'

'Promise not to scratch?'

'Only gently.'

Much later I crept down to the kitchen to make myself a jam-sandwich. Jock was there, moodily eating baked beans. He bore all the marks of a servant who has lost heavily at dominoes. We did not speak. I, for one, was thinking.

3

Who hath given, who hath sold it thee,
Knowledge of me?
Has the wilderness told it thee?
Hast thou learnt of the sea?
Hast thou communed in spirit with night? have the winds
taken counsel with thee?

Hertha

Johanna and I do not share a bedroom, still less a bed. To sleep in the same bed with a member of the opposite sex is barbarous, unhygienic, unaesthetic and, in these blessed days of the electric blanket, quite unnecessary. It means, too, that wakefulness in one is visited upon the other partner and, worst of all, it is conducive to carnality in the mornings – terribly bad for the heart and makes you eat too large a breakfast. When I find a woman that I want to spend the whole night with – I mean, including sleep – in the same bed, then I shall know that I'm in love – or senile. Probably, by then, both.

It was in my dressing-room, then, that Jock aroused me on Easter Tuesday. His 'good morning' was no gruffer than usual; there was perhaps hope that he had declared a truce. Nevertheless, I tasted my tea guardedly, for the keenest weapon in Jock's arsenal is to make tea with water *which has not quite boiled*: a fearful revenge, but then Jock is a man of violence, this is why I employ him.

The tea was good. Jock had selected the Assam Flowery BOP from Jackson's *atelier* and had made it with his deftest touch. I beamed upon the honest fellow.

'Jock, today I am to be a member of a posse. Pray lay out for me a suit of Levis, a ten-gallon hat, high-heeled boots, a Winchester '73 rifle and a strong, durable horse.'

'We ain't got none of that, Mr Charlie.'

'Then plus-fours, stout boots and a great cudgel.'

'Right. Am I coming?'

'Not at this stage, but please stay near the telephone until I call.'

'Right. 'Course you know you won't catch him, don't you?'

I gaped.

'Catch whom?'

'The bloke who rogered Mrs Breakspear, of course. Silly bugger, he only had to say please, didn't he?'

'Watch your tongue. Mr Breakspear's a friend of mine.'

'Sorry, Mr Charlie. But everybody . . .'

'Shut up. Anyway, how do you come to have heard of the, er, incident?'

'Girl who delivers the newspapers.'

'But the papers come from Grouville and they're here before eight. How can it have got so far overnight?'

'Jersey,' he said enigmatically.

'Yes. Of course. But what's this about never catching him?'

'Use your common-sense, Mr Charlie. Where are you going to *look*, for one thing?'

'I had been asking myself that, I admit. What was the other thing?'

'*They* say you won't. The Jerseys. *They* know.'

'Hm, yes, that is another thing.'

'Yeah.'

At noon, clad in thick Irish thornproof tweeds and brandishing an ashplant, I clumped in my great boots into the drawing-room at Les Cherche-fuites. George was wearing flannels and a white shirt, Sam was wearing Bermuda shorts and a silk Palm Beach shirt. They gazed at me wonderingly.

'This is only a conference,' George explained gently.

'Oh. I see.'

'Have you brought many beaters?' Sam asked.

'No.'

'But a *loader*, perhaps?'

My riposte was swift as light.

'I usually drink a glass of bottled beer at about this time,' I said, and went out to the kitchen to fetch it.

Back in the drawing-room I noticed a large, ill-assembled man in a blue suit fidgeting on the edge of an upright chair. His head was many sizes too small for his great frame but his hands made up for it; they were like shovels. He proved to be the Centenier, one Hyacinthe le Mignone, and he shook hands with great gentleness, like a man who is afraid of breaking things. His voice was just such a melancholy, long, withdrawing roar as Matthew Arnold used to delight in.

The conference had barely begun, only civilities and things had thitherto been exchanged. The Centenier began to utter.

'Well, Mr Breakspear,' he roared, 'I 'aven't yet turned up anything you could call a positive lead. We 'ave only two known sex-offenders worth the name in this Parish and neither of them seems to fit the bill. One of them has a diseased mind all right, eh? but 'is modus operandi is quite unlike that what your lady has related. 'E is chiefly interested in little girls' bicycle-saddles which we reckon a 'armless hobby for an ageing man, though we keep a sharp eye on 'im, eh? 'E did indeed once coax a liddle lass into a daffodil field but as soon as 'e started getting above 'imself she stuck 'er finger in 'is eye and run and told 'er father, who 'appened to be the Vingtenier and 'urt the old man real nasty; I don't reckon 'e'll try that again, eh?'

This was entrancing stuff, it made me wish that I were a novelist.

'The other one is just a kid of fifteen or so. 'E 'as bin blessed with a unusually large member, which 'e cannot resist showing to respectable women once in a while, eh? None of them 'as ever made a complaint but the boy always comes to me and confesses and tries to wag it at me – says 'e wants me to understand!'

'And do you *look*?' I asked, with a straight face.

'My Chri' no. I tell 'im to show it to the College of Surgeons and give 'im a kick up the arse, eh? I probably seen better anyway,' he added with a betraying modesty.

'The only other possibility,' he went on, 'oh, thanks, I shouldn't really, my wife will give me hell if she smells it on me breath; the only other possibility is some person or persons unknown who in the Spring and early Summer months persists in stealing ladies' knickers from washing lines. But this doesn't sound like a desperate bloke who climbs in windows and takes on strong young ladies, does it? It sounds more like someone addicted to what we call the Solitary Vice. What's more, he always pinches these great big old bloomers, eh? what we used to call bumbags, not the sort of pretty frilly things your lady will likely wear.'

He lapsed into a thoughtful silence, his eyes hooded.

'Get on, man,' barked George.

'So we reckon 'e's not likely from our Parish but where is 'e from then? Trinity's the nearest next Parish and they 'aven't anyone there to compare with us.'

There was a pardonable pride in his voice.

'They got two or three poofs like we all 'ave and a couple of little tarts on the game – Dirty Gertie and Cutprice Alice and them – but they stick to St Helier, where the money is, eh? Oh, and there's a geezer who rings up ladies and goes on about what he fancies doing to them but we all know who 'e is and 'e's a well-liked chap and does no harm, 'e's terrified of 'is wife. And that's it.'

'What about St John's?' said George, levelly.

'Don't reelly know. Lot of savages there, but nothing like this that I've heard of. Old La Pouquelaye, of course, but 'e's just disgusting. Calves, 'e does it with.'

We sat silently; dazed at this revelation of how the other half lives. I felt that life had passed me by.

'Have you talked to the Paid Police?' asked George.

'Of course, sir. They said they were always glad to hear about our country goings-on but they didn't see how they could help. Unless me and my Vingteniers could give them something to work on.'

'Such as?'

'Well, footprints first. Any good ones, they said they'd come and take casts of.'

'No luck, I'm afraid. I've already looked. I sort of landed heavily when pursuing the beggar and must have wiped out his traces under the window. After that he seems to have kept to the gravel. No sign at all.'

'You sure, sir?'

'I helped to form the Réconnaissance Corps in 1942.'

'Ah. I was helping to form the Jersey Resistance just about then meself.'

They gave each other keen, soldierly looks, such as strong men exchange in the works of R. Kipling.

'Then they said about fingerprints and other clues.'

'Bad luck there, too. My wife's maid did the room thoroughly before we were up. Officious bitch. Usually can't get her to empty an ashtray.'

'That's unfortunate, eh?'

'Very. But I don't suppose you have much of a fingerprint file on the Island.'

'Not what you'd call an up-to-date one. Well, the other thing is semen stains. It seems they can get them classified now, like blood.'

'No,' said George.

'So if you could let me have the lady's sheets, or any garments –'

'I said no.'

'Perhaps the doctor took some samples –'

'Positively bloody NO!' George bellowed, quite startling us all.

'Yes, of course, sir. There's a sort of delicacy –'

George stood up.

The Centenier shut up.

'You won't stay to luncheon?' asked George in a voice from the nineteenth century. 'No. Well, I must thank you for all your help. Most kind. You hadn't a hat? No. A fine day, is it not. Goodbye.'

He closed the front door, quite gently. When he was back in the room he eyed us, defying us to grin. At last, he grinned himself.

'The phrase you are groping for,' I said carefully, 'is "Fuck an old rat".'

'Fuck an old rat,' he said. 'A good cavalry expression. The cavalry has its rôle, after all, in modern life.'

Sam seemed to awake from a heavy slumber.

'I could *eat* an old rat,' he said.

'There was half a cold duck in the fridge,' George said apologetically, 'but I'm afraid I ate it last night just after you men had left. Sonia is in no shape for cooking and the maid cannot tell an Aga from an autoclave. Let us go to Bonne Nuit Bay and eat lobsters.'

'But will they let Charlie in?' asked Sam sweetly. 'I mean, he does look just a little *farouche* . . .'

25

I gazed at him thoughtfully. His tongue was ever sharp but lately he seemed to have been gargling with acid.

'I shall go and change,' I said stiffly. 'Please order for me. I shall have a medium-sized hen lobster split and broiled with a great deal of butter, three potato croquettes and a salad made with the hearts of two lettuces. I shall dress the salad myself.'

'Wine?' said Sam.

'Thank you, how kind. I shall drink whatever you offer; your judgement in these matters is famous.'

Over lunch we agreed that very little could be done until we had more information. George set up a fighting-fund of £100: ten £5 bribes to be slipped to gardeners and other venal fellows who might lay their ears to the ground, and five £10 rewards for any of them who brought in concrete information. Larger rewards, he shrewdly pointed out, might well provoke imagination rather than hard news.

We parted at three; I, for one, in that state of tentative eupepsia which only a broiled lobster and a bottle of Gewurtztraminer can bestow, augmented by the fact that Sam had, indeed, paid for the wine.

I drove to St Helier and the Library of the Museum of the *Société Jersiaise*. They said it was private but I murmured the name of a learned Rector and, instantly, red carpets blossomed beneath my feet.

The material I wanted was dispersed and hard to find, for I particularly did not want to enlist the librarian's help, and, when I found it, a great deal was in *Patois Jersiais* and the rest in antique Norman-French. A sample of *Patois* will, I think, give you an idea of the horrors of that tongue: '*S'lou iou que l'vent est quand l'soleit s'couche la séthée d'la S. Miché, ché s'la qu'nous etha l'vent pour l'hivé.*' This is supposed to mean that the direction of the wind at sunset on Michaelmas Day will be the prevailing wind throughout the following winter – a likely story, I must say.

I staggered out into the evening sunshine and the monstrous regiment of tourists with my head buzzing-full of recondite information. It was clear that scholarship of that kind was not for Mortdecai: a specialist was called for. Nevertheless, I now knew a few things about Paisnel which the police didn't. For instance, both he and his china toad had indeed been 'part of something'; something which is supposed to have died three hundred years ago, something almost as nasty as the people who stamped it out – or thought they had.

Johanna was out when I arrived at the flat; she would be playing bridge, the least strenuous of her vices, bless her. With luck she would get home very late and too tired for romps.

I wrote to Hatchards for a copy of *Malleus Maleficarum*, that great compendium of medieval horrors, and begged them, with many an underlining, to see that it was in *English*.

Jock and I, on friendly terms again, feasted in the kitchen on pork chops, fried peas and mashed potatoes, capping them with a *croque-monsieur* in case of night starvation.

Then, aiding digestion with a bottle of Mr Teacher's best and brightest, we watched Bogart and Bergman in *Casablanca*, that flawless pearl of a film. There wasn't a dry eye in the house. If television didn't exist, someone would have to invent it, is what I say.

I was in hoggish slumber when Johanna climbed into my bed, she was glowing with the radiance of a woman who has just won more than eighty pounds from a close friend. She spends at least that sum each month on her breakfast champagne but her pleasure was intense and she tried to communicate it to me in her own special way.

'No, please,' I protested, 'it's very late and I am suffering from Excess at Table.'

'Well at least tell me what happened today,' she pouted. 'Did you catch the Fiend in Human Shape?'

'We didn't look. We've decided that all we can do for the present is lay our ears to the ground and hope for gossip. But we did meet a lovely Centenier who told us all about the local sex-maniacs.'

She listened, saucer-eyed, as I related all I could remember about the neighbourhood satyrs.

'And in St John's,' I ended, 'there's a well-respected man who does it with *calves*: what do you say to that?'

She rolled over on to all fours, her delightful bottom coquettishly raised.

'Mooo?' she asked hopefully.

'Oh, very well.'

4

His speech is a burning fire;
With his lips he travaileth;
In his heart is a blind desire,
In his eyes foreknowledge of death;
He weaves, and is clothed with derision;
Sows, and he shall not reap;
His life is a watch or a vision
Between a sleep and a sleep.

Atalanta

'Jock,' I said to Jock as I sipped the blessed second cup of the true Earl Grey's Blend on the morning of Easter Wednesday. (I suppose there *is* an Easter Wednesday? For my part the only moveable feast which has any charms is the saddle-of-mutton trolley at Simpson's.)

'Jock,' I said, 'although you are but a rough, untutored fellow I have observed in you certain qualities which I prize. For once I do not refer to your heaven-sent gifts with the teapot and the frying-pan but to another, rarer talent.'

He moved his head slightly, so that his glass eye could give me a non-committal look.

'I refer, on this occasion, to your innate ability to get into conversations, eternal friendships and fights with chaps in pubs.'

'Hunh. You gave me a right bad time when I had me last little punch-up, didn't you?'

28

'Yes, well, but that was because you *killed* the chap, wasn't it, and I've told you and told you not to, and you know what it does to my digestion, and I had to tell *fibs* to the police about you having been with me all evening watching Molière on the television and they didn't believe a word of it, did they?'

He gave me his juiciest smile, the one that still frightens even me, the one which exposes a single, long, yellow fang nestling on his liver-hued nether lip.

Be that as it may,' I went on, 'this gift or knack of yours shall now be usefully employed. Here are ten pounds, the finest that the Bailiwick of Jersey can print. You are to lay them out on beer, cider, rum or whatever pleases your actual rebarbative Jerseyman. Do not buy drinks for any but true-born Jerseymen. They are the ones who will know.'

'Know what, Mr Charlie?'

'Know who was where on Easter Monday. Know who is the sort of chap who would climb up a perilous wistaria to slake his lawless lust; know who still takes part in very old-fashioned and naughty revels – and know, perhaps, who keeps a china toad on his, ah, mantelpiece.'

He thought for a minute or two, or at any rate, he frowned and chewed his lip as he has seen other people do when they were thinking.

'I can't ask these Jerseys that sort of stuff. They'd shut up like bloody clams.'

'Don't ask them. Tell them. Tell them what *you* think it's all about. Talk rubbish while you fill their ale-pots. Then watch: see who smiles. Listen: and see who calls you an idiot. Do not hit them; play the mug, let them pull your plonker. Someone will walk into the trap.'

'You mean, do a Les Kellet?'

'Exactly.'

(Les Kellet is a superb wrestler and consummate clown: he seems to stumble about in a happy daze but his stumbles usually occur just when his opponent leaps on him for the *coup de grâce*. He is puzzled and sorry when the opponent shoots through the ropes and lands on his bonce outside the ring. Sometimes he helps the other chap back into the ring, dusts him down, then administers a fearsome forearm smash and the winning pinfall. Sometimes, too, he picks

29

up the referee absent-mindedly and hits the other chap with him. He is very brave and strong and amusing.)

I briefed Jock a little more from the depths of my ignorance and waved him away in the general direction of the tavern doors.

Soon I heard his great motor-bike start up and burble down the lane. I say 'burble' because it's one of those lovely old pre-war Ariel 1,000c.c. machines with four cylinders and Brooklands fishtail exhausts. It is Jock's pride and joy and I find it utterly terrifying.

The pubs would be open and thronged already, they never seem to close in Jersey. (There are frequent flights from Heathrow; book now to avoid disappointment.) I went back to sleep, secure in the knowledge that the matter of liquoring-up the peasantry was in the hands of a mastercraftsman. Going back to sleep is infinitely sweeter than going to sleep in the first place.

I had scarcely closed my eyes, it seemed, before Johanna aroused me – and I use the word 'aroused' with precision. I opened an eye.

'Have you brought tea?' I asked.

'Of course not. You *are* funny, Charlie.'

'In that case, NO, and let me remind you of Uncle Fred and Auntie Mabel who fainted at the breakfast-table.'

'Charlie, it is not the morning, it is past one o'clock. And you don't eat breakfast, you know you don't.'

I fled to the shower but I was too slow, she got in as well. We re-enacted the battle of Custer's Last Stand. Later, I found that it had been only half-past eleven in the morning after all; it's a poor thing if a chap's own wife lies to him, don't you think?

Then she drove us over to Gorey in the East of the Island for a surprise luncheon at 'The Moorings' where the shellfish are very good. Johanna kept on looking at me anxiously as though she feared I might faint at table. On the way home, for some obscure, American reason, she stopped to buy me a huge bottle of multi-vitamin pills.

Jock was still out. Johanna and I sat on the lawn in the sun and drank hock and seltzer. She will not usually drink in the afternoons but I explained that it was Oscar Wilde's birthday and, who knows, it may well have been.

In the evening we went to a dinner-party on the Isle of Alderney, which has been aptly described as 1,500 alcoholics clinging to a rock. It was a delicious dinner but the flight home in Sam's little Piper was terrifying: he smelled of *drink*.

Jock was in the kitchen when we returned. He was by no means drunk by his standards but there was a betraying woodenness about his face and gait which suggested that his Jersey chums had not drunk the ten pounds unassisted.

Johanna, who was 'excused games' as we used to say at Roedean, went to bed.

'Well, Jock, any news?'

'Not really Mr Charlie, but I got a few night-lines laid, you might say. Wasted a bit of time on a bloke who turned out to be a Guernsey: well, I didn't know, did I?'

'I believe they wear a different sort of pullover.'

'Well I'm not a bloody milliner, am I?'

'No, Jock. Press on.'

'Well, some of the Jerseys seemed sort of interested and I reckon one or two of them would have opened up a bit if their mates hadn't bin there. Anyway, I got one of them coming here tomorrow night to play dominoes; I pretended I'd pinched a bottle of your Scotch.'

'*Pretended?*'

'Yeah. Oh, and I took on an old geezer to come and help out in the garden a few hours a week, hope that's all right. He seemed a right old character, met 'im in the pub at Carrefour Selous, the governor there says the old geezer knows every inch of Jersey and never had a bath in 'is life.'

'What a splendid chap he must be, I long to meet him. What is that you are eating?'

'Cormbeef samwidge.'

'With lots of mustard?'

' 'Course.'

'And thickly-sliced onions, I daresay?'

'Right.'

'The bread sounds fresh and crusty.'

'Oh, all right, let me finish this and I'll make you one.'

'How you read my mind!' I marvelled.

'Mr Charlie?'

'Yes, Jock?'

'What's a crappo?'

'I've no idea. Why?'

'Well this Guernsey said it was a matey thing to say to the Jerseys and he put me on to saying it to one of them and the Jersey tried to hit me.'

'*Tried?* Jock, have you been fighting?'

'Nah. I caught his fist and sort of squeezed till he said it was all a mistake and the landlord told him I didn't mean no harm, but when I asked what it meant they got nasty again so I left it alone and bought another round and there was no hard feelings except I think they kicked the Guernsey man up the bum when they got him outside. Funny you don't know what crappo means, I've heard you talk French lovely.'

'*Crapaud!*' I cried.

'Yeah, that's it. Crappo.'

'It's a French word; it means a toad.'

'A toad, eh?'

'Yes. And you say the Jerseys don't like it?'

'They *'ate* it. They reckon it's a diabolical liberty.'

'And "diabolical" may be a better word than you think.'

'Eh?'

'Never mind. Where's that sandwich?'

'Coming. Oh, one other thing I nearly forgot. When I was going on about this raper bloke having a sword painted on his belly, one or two of them sort of nudged each other and the old geezer who's coming to do the garden had a bit of a chuckle too. I didn't ask, I could see they weren't going to let on. Private joke, I reckon. Or p'raps it means something dirty.'

'Perhaps both. I think I detect the distant clash of phallic cymbals.'

'Eh?'

'Yes. Ah, the sandwich. How delicious. I shall take it to bed with me. Good night, Jock.'

'Goo' night, Mr Charlie.'

I know I meant to go and say good night to Johanna, for I realize how much these little civilities mean to the frailer sex, but I dare say I forgot. Even men aren't perfect.

5

Yea, he is strong, thou say'st,
A mystery many-faced,
The wild beasts know him and the wild birds flee;
The blind night sees him, death
Shrinks beaten at his breath,
And his right hand is heavy on the sea:
We know he hath made us, and is king;
We know not if he care for anything.

To Victor Hugo

Nothing really happened the following day except that, in the morning, my liver and I could by no means seem to get along together. I drank Milk of Magnesia, Alka-Seltzer and Eno's Fruit Salts, in that order, until my stomach was a mere cave of the winds and the waters, but to no avail.

'You need a drink, Mr Charlie,' said Jock, with rough compassion.

'Do you really think that might help?'

'Bloody sure it would.'

I had one, just to please Jock and, do you know, he was perfectly right. He *knows*, you see.

Nothing really had happened in the newspapers that day, either, except that some Arabs had murdered some Jews, some Jews had retaliated on some Arabs, some Indians had perfected an atomic bomb for dropping on Pakistanis and various assorted Irishmen had

33

murdered each other in unpleasant ways. You really have to hand it to God, you know, he has terrific staying-power. Jehovah against Mohammed, Brahma against Allah, Catholic against Protestant: religion really keeps the fun going, doesn't it. If God didn't exist the professional soldiers would have to invent him, wouldn't they?

Nothing nearly so warlike had happened in Jersey, except that an old lady had found a neighbour lifting potatoes which he had inadvertently planted in land which had since been adjudged hers, so she had raised the ancient *Clameur de Haro*, which dates back to Rollo, the first Norman Lord of the Island. What you have to do to raise the *Clameur* is to collect a witness or two, drop on your knees and shout '*Haro! Haro! Haro! A l'aide, mon prince! On me fait tort!*' Whereupon the wrongdoer has to stop whatever wrong he is doing and the whole situation freezes until it can be sorted out at a high level. You have to be pretty sure of yourself to raise the *Clameur*; they take it seriously in Jersey and, even if you are technically in the right, you can find yourself 'amerced' for a good round fine if you have been wasting the court's time on spite or trivialities – or if your plea doesn't fit the conditions for proper clamouring.

Nothing happened chez Mortdecai, either, except that the new gardener appeared. His name may well have been something like Henri Le Pieton Gastineau, but his native wood-notes wild were blemished by a complete absence of teeth and, even when he took them out of his pocket and burnished them on the seat of his trousers before popping them into his mouth, it was hard to achieve a real communion of souls. What I did establish was that he wanted '*quat' louis les sept heures*' which my razor-like brain converted into 57 pence per hour – a fair rate if he happened to be capable of toil. As it turned out he was a positive dynamo. 'Flash', our tame slug, tried playing head-gardener and bullying him, but got nowhere: he then played his last card and offered his notice – which to his intense chagrin we accepted.

Nothing was new except that it was the First of May, which was Pinch-Bum Day when I was at my dame-school but is now known as Labour Day, when portly, well-paid Trades Union officials persuade lean, ill-paid Trades Union dues-payers to march about the streets saying 'hooray' for excellent reasons of their own. They carry beautiful woven banners each of which would keep a starving docker's wife in Bingo cards for a week. But I digress.

Nothing happened personally to me except that a funny thing happened to me at the Pistol and Rifle Club which I always attend on the first Thursday of the month.

I had decided to give my old and beautiful .455 Smith and Wesson Military and Police Model of 1902 an airing. The men there teased me about it as ever; most of them have amazing small-bore weapons with tailored handles and changeable sights, but they know that I can still make the pop-up man-sized target look pretty sick at standard Olympic range. Although I say it as shouldn't. It weighs 2¾ pounds fully loaded and the barrel is 6 inches long; using the high-load, nickel-jacketed military ammunition it can punch holes in a brick wall and it makes a deafening and highly satisfying noise. Everyone with an organ-inferiority should have one. (Like, say, Bach?)

A nice police-sergeant made his usual joke about it, saying that if I bought it a pair of wheels I could get a commission in the Royal Artillery, and then the funny thing that happened to me was that he asked me if I had my bullets specially cast.

'Yes, a nice chap in London,' I said.

'Lead?' he asked. I was puzzled.

'Of course, lead, what else?'

'No, nothing, just asking. There's a bloke here on the Island who'll cast them in *anything*, if ever you need it.'

'Well, thanks,' I said, still puzzled.

That was the funny thing that happened.

I didn't give it any more thought. I was too preoccupied with what always preoccupies me on the First of May: the essential *swindle* of all English months and May in particular. Why have we let the poets and, no doubt, politicians, sell us all this rubbish about the months? I mean, May conjures up the vision of happy, sun-burned maidens prancing on the village green and retiring at dusk to the nearest hedgerow to be turned into happy, sunburned, unmarried mothers-to-be; but the truth is that the pallid and pimply village maiden of today is waving her lumpish hips in a discotheque in the nearby town, munching a contraceptive pill while the rain roars down outside and the Babycham fizzes in its glass. Anyone braving a hedgerow in an English May, even in full oilskins, courts both pneumonia and insecticide-poisoning. Perhaps the only month which one can depend on is January, when the cold is always as promised and one can still sometimes hear the ring of skates on the frozen tarn and, if one is lucky, the shriek of a drowning skater.

When I say that nothing happened that day, I did not mean to suggest that nothing happened that night. Much did.

Johanna was watching lovingly as I mopped up the gravy of one of the finest coq-au-vins (coqs au vin?) of my life with a huge crust of crusty bread when the telephone rang.

'Tell them I'm out,' I snarled, 'or dead, or bankrupt, I don't care; but I'm not answering that machine, tell the Post Office to take it away in the morning, we'll be better without it.'

'It's for you, Mr Charlie,' said Jock a moment later.

'Look, are you incapable of . . .' I started, but then I saw Jock's expression. I went to the telephone, wiping my lips. Sam was on the line. It was a Sam I had never heard.

'Get round here, Charlie, fast. It's Violet.'

'You mean . . .?'

'Yes. Get here.'

I got. To be exact, I told Jock to get there on his motor-bike, carrying his low friend (perhaps glad to be free from the domino-lesson) on the pillion; while I bundled Johanna into the Mini. I knew she was probably safe from rapists (they rarely have the stamina to strike twice in one night) but I knew, too, that all women love to comfort their frailer sisters in adversity.

At La Gouluterie, Sam was in the courtyard, giving Jock and his domino-friend orders in the ugliest voice I have ever heard. He sent them off and turned to me.

'Charlie, send Johanna up to Violet; the doctor and police are coming. Jock is patrolling on his motor-bike towards Belle Etoile Bay and back via Wutherings; his friend is working the fields – don't shoot him by accident. You will drive me to Sion and I'll work back from there. Then you will drive like hell to St John's Church and come slowly back without lights. Are you armed?'

'Naturally.'

'Then grab anyone in trousers; if they can't give a wholly satisfactory account of themselves force them into the car. I'll pay any fines for wrongful arrest. Got all that? Then let's go.'

'What's George doing?'

'Nothing. They're out.'

With that he opened a gun-case and assembled his beautiful Churchill XXV shotgun with a brutality which made me wince. Off we sped. We saw no one. I left him at Sion, drove fast to St John's, crawled back, stopping to look and listen from time to time. One party of drunks arguing bitterly about football. One burly she-hitch-hiker from Wigan: she hadn't seen anyone. One sinister chap who was a rapist if ever I saw one but he already had a local maiden with him: the dirty look she gave me indicated that she was actually *hoping* to lose her maiden status even if it meant braving a hedgerow and that I was delaying things. Her swain claimed to have heard, ten minutes earlier, a large motor-bike driving towards the *Route Militaire* very fast, then stopping. A few minutes later it had started up again and gone North, much more slowly. That had evidently been Jock: this lad, for all his saucy looks, was a good witness. His restless sacrifice was tugging at his sleeve, saying –

'Ow, come on Norman, it's none of our business,' and so forth, so I attracted his interest by taking out the fat little Banker's Special revolver and spinning the cylinder, as though to check the load. This fascinated him, it was the Wild West come true.

'You the police, then, eh?'

I chuckled fatly.

'No, no. It's a little more important than that,' I said, in what he may well have taken for a Secret Service voice. 'Have you seen or heard anyone else – on foot perhaps?'

'No.'

'Would you have noticed, do you think?'

'Bloody right. I'm keeping me ear open for the young lady's dad, ain't I?'

'Yes, of course. Quite right. Well, thanks for your help.'

I was almost at the car when he made a chirruping noise and beckoned me. I went back to him.

'Funny you should ask that, mister. There's a bugger in the field of taters behind us, just come in through the hedge. I can't see him but I can hear him.'

'Ow, Norman, it's none of our business, etc.'

'Belt up, daft cow.' (How courtship has changed since our days, has it not?)

Norman and I stole into the field and, sure enough, a bugger was, indeed, tip-toeing through the taters. When the time and place were ripe I swept his feet from under him and Norman dived. The man squealed, cursed foully, kicked and clawed. When we had subdued him he proved to be Jock's domino-pupil, much chagrined: about five pounds' worth as it turned out. I gave Norman a sweetener too, and he eagerly proffered his name and address in case I ever needed any more deeds of derring-do.

The domino-man and I arrived at La Gouluterie at the very moment when George's Rover arrived with George and Sam, who had been picked up on the *Route Militaire*. Jock swept up on his Ariel before we had entered the house. Nothing to report, from anyone.

Except the doctor. He didn't like any part of this; he was a measles-and-mumps man and his mask of professional confidence was slipping. Much of what he said was for Sam's ear alone but we others could see Sam's face twist and darken as he listened. The professional murmuring went on, while Sam ground his teeth. George looked detachedly into space and I fidgeted. It was not, as the children say nowadays, my scene at all.

The situation was so fraught that Sam almost forgot to give the doctor his ritual glass of brown sherry before speeding him off on some other errand of mercy. (He was probably an excellent chap, a credit to Apothecaries' Hall, but I find it hard to trust doctors with large, unhygienic moustaches. 'He that sinneth, let him fall into the hands of the Physician', I always say.)

Johanna came downstairs looking troubled: Violet had at last succumbed to the massive dose of sedative that the doctor had hosed into her (would you believe 15 millilitres of paraldehyde?) but she was in a pretty sorry state. We all went into conference and the story-until-now emerged as follows.

The assailant had apparently entered the house through the pantry window. Violet had been in her bedroom, taking off her make-up before showering. She had been clad only in those sensible woolly knickers which girls like Violet always wear. Suddenly a hideous shape had appeared in her dressing-table mirror – only for a second, because the light went out an instant later.

Sam had been in his study, which is lined with books, even the doors, which make it virtually sound-proof; but in any case Johanna doesn't think Violet would have screamed, she would have been petrified with terror.

The rapist had been rough, to put it mildly, and had savaged Violet both here and there. The Marquis de Sade could have taken his correspondence course profitably. He seemed to have been motivated more by hatred than lust. Violet had babbled incoherently to Johanna for a few minutes before lapsing into a clenched sort of silence and the few cogent bits which Johanna could remember were:

'He stank horridly, like a goat.'

'He smelt of grease, but nasty.'

'He was wearing a horrid mask, it smelt of rubber.'

'He hated me.'

'He had a sword painted on his tummy.' (In Violet's Noddy-world, even mad rapists have tummies, not bellies. Enid Blyton, Enid Blyton, how much we all owe you!)

'He had spikes on his arms.' (George and I looked at each other, this was straight from the Beast of Jersey case-book.) 'He kept on saying beastly things, they were in a weird language – no, not patois – but I could tell they were beastly things.'

'His hands were all covered with earth, they *hurt* me.'

The really nasty thing, however, the thing that had made her at last scream, was that, after the fiend had slid out of the window, she had felt something cold and wet, high up between her thighs.

It had wriggled.

'It was a frog, for Christ's sake,' said Sam disgustedly, 'the man is clearly insane.'

'A *frog?*' I asked.

'That's what I said.'

'Sam, was it sort of greeny yellow with long hind-legs?'

'God blast it, Charlie, you do try a man's patience. I was in no mood to look at the thing's legs. I just snatched it up and threw it.'

'Where?'

He half rose, murder in his eyes, then thought better of it.

'I think I threw it into the waste-paper basket,' he said, in the strangled sort of voice you use when you want people to know that no further questions will be answered.

'Johanna,' I said, 'will you please go and find it?'

She went. She found it. It wasn't greenish-yellow with long legs, it was brown and naevous and squat.

'It's a *toad*,' I said.

39

'So?'

'Nothing.'

'Sod you too.'

'I think there is no one here,' I said gently, 'who would not be the better for a drink.'

Sam got up in a robotical sort of way and started to dish out the liquor; courteously assisted by me, for I feared that, in his distress, I might receive the wrong brand of Scotch, which would have quite spoiled my evening.

We guzzled our drinks silently, respectfully, like distant cousins helping themselves to baked ham after the funeral.

'Oh, one other thing Violet said,' said Johanna. We stopped guzzling: Johanna can make most people stop doing most things when she chooses, without even raising her voice. I wonder why that is.

'Yes, that's it,' she went on, 'she said she recognized the man's voice.'

'What?' shouted two of the three of us.

'Yes.' Her lovely eyes danced innocently, aimlessly around the room, alighting on everything and everyone except Sam. 'Well, to be exact, in the midst of some alarming chatter about her mother and so on she suddenly said, "I could tell that voice anywhere, *anywhere*; I couldn't be wrong" or something like that.' She paused; too long.

'Well, who, for God's sake?' George growled at last.

'She didn't say. Perhaps she only meant that she would know it again.'

My ensuing silence was puzzled; George's and Sam's silences appeared to be merely disgusted, but you never can tell.

Why I was puzzled was because Johanna was using the warm, true, *real* voice which she only uses when she is lying. Which isn't often, naturally; with all those looks and all that money, why should she bother?

I had the feeling, intensely, that a lot of complicated reactions were taking place in the room which I wasn't quite following because I didn't know what I was looking for. I'm not at all sure that Johanna knew, either, but it was clear to me that she was less at sea than I was. I gave up after a while with a mental 'heigh-ho' or two and applied myself to Sam's Scotch.

Like a good guest, I saw to it that Sam, too, ingested enough of the delicious fluid to ensure him a good night's rest in spite of everything; then we slunk away.

Johanna went to bed; kissing me but not fondly.

Jock was up, brewing 'Sergeant-Major's' which is the sort of tea you used to relish when coming off guard-duty in a January dawn: it is the cheapest Indian tea *boiled-up* with sugar and condensed milk. It is not at all like tea as you and I know it but it is very good indeed. I gazed at it longingly.

'You don't want none of that, Mr Charlie,' said Jock, 'you'll be wanting to get off to boo-boo's.' I glared.

'Have you been listening at keyholes?' I demanded.

' 'Course not. I've heard Madam use the phrase in public, frequently.'

'Ugh.'

'Yeah.'

I turned away.

'Mr Charlie,' he said.

'Yes?'

'That mate of mine I was teaching dominoes – the one you scragged.'

'Yeah.'

'He was going on about toads. He reckons the Jerseys think a lot of them, which is why they don't like being called them.'

'You put that beautifully, Jock.'

'Yeah. He got on about it because the old geezer who's come to do the garden just buried one alive in a pickle-jar to make the flowers grow.'

'To make the flowers grow? Do go on.'

'They all do it here, he reckons. It doesn't seem to bother the toads, they're nearly always alive when they dig them up in the autumn. Funny, innit? You'd think they'd get hungry.'

'Or thirsty?'

'Yeah. Anyway, a lot of the Jerseys, specially the old ones, reckon a toad's sort of holy and they don't like people taking the mickey about it.'

I took a gulp of his tea.

'You should put a little rum in this,' I advised.

'Well, I haven't got any rum, have I?'

'Do you mean you have forgotten how to pick the lock of the drinks cupboard?'

He maintained an injured silence. I went to fetch the rum, while he made some more Sergeant-Major's.

When we were firmly seated astride the tea and certain Welsh Rabbits which Jock had conjured up to help it down, I waxed informative, a vice of mine which I can by no means cure.

'Jock,' I said, 'did you know that for fifteen centuries people believed that the toad had a precious jewel inside its skull?'

'Reelly?' he said. 'What give them that idea, then?'

'Pliny or Aristotle or one of those chaps who wrote it in a book.'
Jock munched and golluped awhile.

'Well, didn't nobody think to chop one open and take a look?'

'Not as far as I know.'

'Fucking ignorant, all them wops, aren't they,' he said, obscurely.
I couldn't find it in my heart to contradict him.

'He went on about hares, too,' Jock went on. 'Seems there aren't supposed to be any hares on the Island but a few years back there was a right big bugger seen and the farmers reckoned it sucked all the milk out of them funny little cows they have here. So they laid up for it and shot it and better-shot it but it wasn't no use, so one of them put a silver button in his gun and shot it in the bum and the hare goes off limping and the next day this creepy old tart who lives nearby has a bandage on her leg.'

'That is probably one of the oldest stories in the world,' I told him, for indeed it is.

I was too tired to take a shower that night: all I wanted was to go to boo-boo's. I brushed my teeth, of course. As I did so I realized why the nice chap at the Pistol and Rifle Club had been so keen on introducing me to the chap who would cast bullets in anything.

Silver was what he had had in mind.

6

I said 'she must be swift and white,
And subtly warm, and half perverse,
And sweet, like sharp soft fruit to bite,
And like a snake's love lithe and fierce.'
Men have guessed worse.

Felise

We had another conference the next morning. Sonia, it seemed, was bearing up and getting about a little, but Violet's case was worse: she had quite stopped speaking and, although she followed you with her eyes, she moved no other part of herself. Sam had got one spoonful of Brand's celebrated Calves' Foot Jelly into her; the second time she had bitten the spoon. After that she wouldn't open her mouth at all. The doctor had mumbled about some sort of psychotic withdrawal which he himself clearly wasn't on very good terms with, and had given her another generous needleful of sedative.

'He didn't quite say "go on taking the tablets",' said Sam, 'but you could see the words on the tip of his tongue. If she hasn't snapped out of it tomorrow I'm getting a second opinion.'

We all nodded and made kindly murmuring sounds, except George who said 'bloody swine' several times.

Sam asked me if I could recommend a good pistol and how should he go about getting one. I told him, and advised a good vintage piece which would be an investment. He didn't seem too interested in

43

that aspect, he wanted something which could be depended upon to punch large and painful holes into rapists.

'Calm yourself,' I urged. 'The best and most modern pistol won't make even a tiny hole in anyone at whom it is not accurately pointed. Most pistols are only for frightening people and making loud noises. The thing is to have it *handy*. Chaps like you and me only need a pistol perhaps once in our lives' – I wasn't being quite truthful there – 'but then we want it in a great hurry indeed. Take my advice and buy a capable, vintage one which you can make a profit on when all this has died down. There is, for instance, a very splendid old Mauser 7.65 mm not five miles away, which can be bought for £150; it's the sort with a wooden scabbard which clips onto the pistol-butt to form a stock and transforms it into a small carbine. It is a most reliable pistol and if you can point it straight it will knock an ox over at half a mile. It is also rather a beautiful object in an ugly sort of way.' He grumbled a bit but took my advice and the Mauserchap's telephone number.

'Yes, yes,' said George, 'that's all very well about the small-arms issue but this is supposed to be an O-Group and we should be doing an Appreciation of the Situation.'

(Those of you who haven't had the luck to serve in the Army should be told that an O-Group is a conference called by an infantry leader below field rank who is finally facing the fact that he is lost and wants his junior officers and senior NCOs to admit that they, too, are lost. An O-Group is always held out of ear-shot of the men, naturally, although the men have known that their officers were lost *hours* before the O-Group is summoned; their idea of a good officer is simply one who calls an O-Group at a time when they want *tea*. Soldiers, up to and, sometimes, including the rank of major, are capital chaps: join *now* – you're too late to have a crack at the Japs but the Irish are good for years yet.)

'I have here,' said George in an efficient sort of voice, 'a list of all nubile women within a mile's radius of this house. I propose we lie out at night, turn and turn about, watching their houses and ready to blow the arse off the filthy hog when he next tries to, er, strike.'

'George,' I said gently. 'George? Who furnished you with this list?'

'The Centenier – he spent hours with his Vingteniers drawing it up.' I let one of those long silences develop, so that all of us could see the daftness of that. Then I said:

'Good. Yes. But we are only three, you know, and have premises and wives of our own to guard – and we don't really know the terrain awfully intimately. More to the point, if you kill a chap even in your own *house* nowadays, with one of his fists in your safe and the other in your wife, you're facing a murder charge and the court will be told by hired psychiatrists that the offender is a poor, disturbed lad who has been upset by a nasty film he saw at the Odeon last week but he's a lovely son to his old mother. Old mothers are marvellous in the witness box, born actors every one, they can even make policemen weep, I've seen it, it's as good as the television. They would give you a very bad time.'

George snarled and gargled a while; he wasn't very cogent but we got the impression that, if he were let loose for a few hours with a Vickers Medium Machine-Gun, the world would be a better place and all potential rapists would be queuing up in Cathedral Closes, applying for jobs as counter-tenors.

Sam and I watched him curiously: I think we both felt that this was not the quiet, capable George we both knew and, in some sort, respected – the George whose most interesting feature was his dullness. We put it down, I suppose, to his recent ordeal and Sam doubtless, although he was showing a surprisingly better front to the world, had a fellow-feeling for him. (I myself gave up having fellow-feelings in my last term at school because I was working hard for University entrance; I like to think that I am a *prude* at heart.)

'I think,' I said, when the noise had died down, 'that I'd better go to Oxford.'

Sam mustered a flash of his old spirit.

'Is this really the best time to consider completing your education, Charlie? Is the call of the cloisters suddenly so strong? What will you read – Divinity?'

'Tush,' I replied. 'I shall go and see my old tutor, who knows more about witchcraft, demonology and kindred nonsense than any man living. It is perfectly clear that we have a disgusting situation here where some vile sub-human is committing outrages for ancient and nasty reasons which we do not comprehend. We cannot stamp him out until we know what he thinks he is doing, and why. I shall go to ask my old tutor. Has anyone any better suggestions?'

No one had any better suggestions.

'My own wife,' I went on, 'has not yet, to my best knowledge, been ravished, so you will see that my mission is pretty disinterested. In the circumstances, and since giving hospitality to dons in Oxford comes wickedly dear, I fancy you may care to split my expenses with me.'

They made fumbling gestures in the direction of their cheque-book pockets but I waved them away.

'Payment by results,' I said. 'If we get any good of my trip I shall submit an expense-sheet.'

'But what about Johanna?' came a tragic voice from half-way up the stairs. It was Sonia: pallid, voluminously wrappered, with just a tactful hint of make-up here and there which most chaps – *nice* chaps – would not have noticed. We all leaped to our feet and surged about getting her chairs, cushions, foot-stools and assorted restoratives. (I made a slight restorative for myself while I was about it, for George did not seem to be on form as a host that night.)

'What about Johanna?' she asked again, 'hadn't she better stay here while you're away so that I can protect her?'

I looked at her kindly.

'You're very kind,' I said, 'but Jock, too, is no slouch in the art of defence. They call it Martial Arts nowadays but when Jock was at Borstal it was known, quite simply, as a "flying drop-kick at the wedding-tackle". I'd back Jock against the finest Kung-fu artist ever groomed by Mr Metro-Goldwyn. He has a gift for it, you see.'

She nodded wisely. She knows she's not clever but she thinks I am, poor deluded bitch.

'Yes, but d'you trust the chap?' asked George.

This annoyed me but I decided I should give a civil answer.

'Jock is true as steel,' I said carefully. 'He has been in love with Shirley Temple since he was fourteen and will not lightly change. He is no butterfly. Second, he owes me a favour or perhaps two and crooks like Jock hold that sort of thing much more sacred than honest men do. Third – and I know this sounds absurd – I am the only man that Jock is afraid of.'

Sam and George shifted uneasily in their seats, they didn't know how to cope with rubbish like that. Sonia said:

'Oh, I think that's absolutely beautiful. I mean, to have a relationship like that, I mean, based on wonderful mutual um . . .'

I looked at her kindly again. Perhaps a little kindlier than last time. You see, we anti-feminists don't dislike women in the least; we prize, cherish, and pity them. We are compassionate. Goodness, to think of the poor wretches having to waddle through life with all those absurd fatty appendages sticking out of them; to have all the useful part of their lives made miserable by the triple plague of constipation, menstruation and parturition; worst of all, to have to cope with these handicaps with only a kind of fuzzy half-brain – a pretty head randomly filled, like a tiddly-winks cup, with brightly-coloured scraps of rubbish – why, it wrings the very heart with pity. You know how your dog sometimes gazes anguishedly at you, its almost human eyes yearning to understand, longing to communicate? You remember how often you have felt that it was on the very brink of breaking through the barrier and joining you? I think that's why you and I are so kind to women, bless 'em. (Moreover, you scarcely ever see them chasing cats or fouling the footpaths.)

'Yes,' I answered her.

Just as we were leaving, Sonia rushed out to the door, still playing the mobled queen.

'Charlie,' she cried, 'will someone look after your dear little canary while you're away?'

'Probably,' I said, vaguely.

'What my old nanny used to say,' grumbled George, 'was that people shouldn't have pets if they weren't prepared to look after them properly.'

'Just what I always say about wives,' I answered brightly. Well, perhaps it wasn't in the best of taste. I never signed any promises about good taste, I'd as soon join the Temperance League.

Johanna went to bed without saying good night. Jock was out, probably hitting people, he never tires of it. I didn't worry about that, he's careful now: people he quarrels with usually walk away – carrying their teeth in their hat. I made some telephone calls to travel-agents and old Oxford tutors then went sulkily to bed, taking with me a volume of Beatrix Potter to comfort my sad heart; it was *The Tale of Mrs Tiggywinkle*, it never fails to please.

7

God is buried and dead to us,
Even the spirit of earth,
Freedom; so have they said to us,
Some with mocking and mirth,
Some with heartbreak and tears;
And a God without eyes, without ears,
Who shall sing of him, dead in the birth?

To Walt Whitman in America

I took the noon flight for Heathrow the next day. I'm not one of the jet-set, more of the biplane set, Johanna says, but I don't at all mind flying except in those terrifying little planes where you sit in the open behind the driver and have to rap on his helmet if you want to tell him to slow down a bit. This was a large, experienced-looking craft and it said on the side that its engines came from the Rolls-Royce stable, most reassuring. Two Jersey worthies whom I know slightly took the seats beside me and, when we were air-borne, I ordered three large gins-and-tonic with my customary munificence. The hostess asked me if I wanted them all in one glass; I believe she was being *pert*.

You don't have to go right into London nowadays if you're headed West: an airlines bus takes you from Heathrow to Reading quite painlessly and trains thence to Oxford, where Dryden, my old tutor, hoves, are plentiful.

Goodness, have you *seen* Oxford Station since they did it up? It's

48

quite amazingly smart and modern and not much more than twice as inconvenient as it was before.

Something quite dreadful happened to me as I stood outside the station waiting for Dryden: a leprous creature, clad in filthy tatters, beard matted and barbaric necklaces jingling, shambled up to me, mopping and mowing, his demeanour both piteous and threatening.

'Be off with you!' I quavered valiantly, brandishing my umbrella. 'I shall not submit to your mugging; I happen to be a personal friend of the station-master, aye, and of the Warden of All Souls, too!'

'Mr Mortdecai?' he fluted in the purest Wykehamist tones. 'My name's Francis, I'm a pupil of Dr Dryden, he's asked me to pick you up, he can't come himself, he's got the squitters. *I've* got the crabs, if you want to know,' he added gloomily. 'And a tutorial and two demos tomorrow.'

I fumbled around in my word-bag for a while.

'How do you do?' I said at length.

He took charge of my suitcase and led me to about five thousand pounds' worth of Italian GT motor-car in which we vroomed painlessly towards the dreaming-spires section of the city. I didn't know quite what to chat about, it's the generation gap I suppose. He was extraordinarily civil and, on closer inspection, as clean as can be. I think he was just boasting about the crabs.

Scone College, my *alma mater*, hadn't changed a bit except that the outside was richly adorned with huge painted words such as 'PEACE', 'SHIT', 'TROTSKY LIVES' and similar sentiments. I thought it something of an improvement, for it took one's eyes off the architecture. Fred was on duty in the Porter's Lodge as he had been when I was there last: he remembered me well and said that I owed him half a sovereign in connection with some long-forgotten horse-race. I wasn't taken in, but I coughed up.

My rooms were ready for me and quite habitable, except that the undergraduate incumbent (this was in the vacation, you see) had pinned up a poster of a little fat black chap called Maharaj ji Guru in such a position that it smirked at the bed. I couldn't move the chap's poster, naturally, so I moved the bed. Bathed and changed, I still had half an hour to spend before I could report at the Senior Common Room where Dryden would, if recovered, meet me and take me to dinner at High Table, so

I strolled over to the Buttery. On the lawn where, in the brave days, we used to play croquet some forty tatterdemalions were squatting silently – a sorry sight. No doubt they were meditating or protesting; they certainly weren't having any fun. As I strolled past them in my exceedingly beautiful dinner jacket I raised a hand in benediction.

'Peace!' I said.

'Shit!' said a spokesman.

'Trotsky lives!' I answered stoutly. You see, you *can* communicate with young people if you take the trouble to learn their lingo.

'Hallo, Mr Mortdecai,' said Henry, the buttery steward, 'have you been away?'

'No, no, no,' I said, 'I was here only seven years ago.'

'So you were, sir. End of a Trinity term it was, I fancy, and you were rude to one of those Hungarian persons that are all over the place now – I can't ever say their names, they always seem to come out rude-sounding when I try.'

'I know just what you mean, Henry. And I'm dying of thirst.'

He really did remember me, for he reached down one of the battered pewter quarts from which we giants used to sup our ale in the olden days. I strolled outside with my tankard so that I could pour half its contents surreptitiously onto the lawn, for I am not the man I was.

'I suppose you find that sort of thing a bit galling, don't you, Henry?' I said, waving my hand towards the solemn sit-in on the lawn.

'Oh, I dunno. I've been here all my life, as well you know. They're not much different from your year, or any year. When I first come here it was top hats and frock-coats on Sunday and parading up and down the Broad Walk; then it was riding-breeches and fox-terriers; then it was Oxford bags and *bull*-terriers. After the war it was them blue demob suits, then tweed jackets and flannels; then straw bashers and blazers come back in and then it was jeans and bare feet and now it's beards and beads and probably tomorrow it'll be top hats again. Only thing I got against this lot is they will eat chocolate-bars with their little gills of beer, and they spend half their money on the french-letter machine in the Junior Common Room. They should be drinking their beer and rowing their boats and learning their books; there's plenty of time for all that sex when they've got their degrees.'

'Just so,' I said. I bade him good night, donned my gown and set sail for the SCR.

Dryden was profuse in his apologies for not having met me at the station.

'I do hope Margate found you without difficulty?'

'Margate? No, it was a rum chap called Francis.'

'Yes, that's right, Francis Margate. A *very* nice boy. Brightest Viscount I've taught for years.'

'I hope your, ah, squitters are better, John? Your pupil seemed to be concerned about you.'

'Oh, goodness, they don't trouble me, I've had them for years, it's the port here, d'you see, worst port in Oxford, don't know why I stay. I've had splendid offers from all sorts of places, Sussex, Lancaster, Uganda – all sorts of places.'

'They all sound much the same to me. What, in fact, did prevent you from meeting me?'

'Oh, I had luncheon at one of those women's colleges, can't recall the name, they get you frightfully drunk, you probably know, shocking lot, boozers every one. So I felt a little *tired* after luncheon and Francis hadn't his essay ready so I offered to let him meet you instead.'

'Just so,' I said. (I find that I say 'just so' often in Oxford, I wonder why that is?)

He then gave me a *filthy* glass of sherry without a word of apology and led me up to the Warden so that I might pay my respects. I paid them.

'How nice,' the Warden said with apparent civility, 'to see an old member.'

To this day I cannot be sure whether it was a gibe or simply an unfortunate turn of phrase.

I strayed around the Common Room until I found a hideous pot-plant which seemed to deserve my sherry. A moment later, we formed the usual sort of procession and shuffled off to Hall, High Table and dinner. High Table was much as it has always been, except for the cut of the dinner-jackets and the absurd youthfulness of the dons, but a glance over my shoulder into the bear-pit of Hall made me shudder. Two hundred shaggy Tom-a-Bedlams with their

51

molls and doxies were scrambling and squabbling around a row of stainless-steel soup-kitchen counters, snapping and snarling like Welsh Nationalists in committee, or Italian press-photographers in pursuit of an adulterous Royal. Every few moments one of them would break out of the *mêlée*, guarding a plate heaped with nameless things and chips, which he would savage at the table, cursing and belching the while. The long oak tables bore none of the ancient silver of my youth – they have to keep it locked up nowadays – but there were long, proud lines of bottles of Daddie's Favourite Sauce – and jolly nice it is too, I dare say. But I turned away with a shudder and dipped a reluctant spoon into the Mock Turtle before me. (You can tell how even the memory of it all upsets me if you note that I started the last sentence with a conjunction, a thing I never do.)

You must not think that I am carping when I say that dinner was five courses of poisonous ordure: I expected it and would have been disturbed if it had been good. High Table dinner in Oxford, as perhaps you know, is always in inverse ratio to the brains-content of the College which offers it. Scone is a very brainy College indeed. If you want a good tuck-in in Oxford you have to go to places like Pembroke, Trinity or St Edmund Hall, where they play rugger and hockey and things like that and, if you're spotted reading a book, someone takes you aside and has a chat with you.

No, what really spoiled my evening was that Scone had gone in for the ultimate gimmick and acquired a she-don. She resembled nothing so much as a badly-tied bundle of old bits of string; her smile was the bitter, clenched rictus of a woman pretending to enjoy natural childbirth and we disliked each other on sight to our mutual satisfaction. She was not wearing a bust-bodice or 'bra', that was clear; her blouse was gallantly taking the strain at about the level of her navel.

I couldn't say anything, could I – as a mere Old Member I was only a guest and she was listening intently – but I met the Warden's eye and gave him a long, level look. He smiled sheepishly, a sort of qualified apology.

After dinner, in the Common Room, Dryden mischievously introduced us.

'Gwladys,' he said with relish. 'Charlie Mortdecai has been dying to meet you.'

'*Bronwen,*' she said curtly. Clearly, Dryden had used that gambit before.

'Enchanted,' I exclaimed in the *galant* voice which I hoped would most enrage her, 'it's high time this stuffy old place had a few pretty faces to brighten it up.'

She turned on me that particularly nasty look which your breakfast kipper gives you when you have a hang-over.

'And what's your field?' I asked.

'Sexual Sociometrics.'

'I might have guessed,' I replied archly. She turned away. Never let a day go by without making an enemy, is what I say, even if it's only a woman.

'You have made a conquest,' murmured Dryden in my ear.

'Have you any whisky in your rooms?'

'Only Chivas Regal.'

'Then let us go there.'

His room are the best set in Scone: there are *boiseries* and a pair of bookcases only rivalled by those in the Pepysian Library in Cambridge and a certain house in Sussex, whose name escapes me. Moreover, he has a bathroom of his own, an unheard-of luxury in Scone, where the *corpus sanum* -- or *vile* -- runs a very bad second to the *mens sana*. (The story goes that, long ago, when it was first proposed in the College *concilium* that bathrooms should be provided for undergraduates, an ancient life-fellow protested in piping tones that the lads couldn't possibly need such things: 'Why, they're only here for eight weeks at a time!' But then came the strange late-Victorian epoch, shot through with obscure guilts, when the English – whom Erasmus had named as the grubbiest race in Europe – found that nothing would do but that they must scrub themselves from head to foot whenever they could spare a moment from smartening up Fuzzy-Wuzzy and other Breeds Without The Law. There are three times as many undergraduates in Scone now, and the bathrooms are just as few, but now no one seems to mind any more.)

'Well now,' said Dryden, when the beaded bubbles of Chivas Regal were winking at the brim, 'I gather that you have taken up the worship of Wicca and find that it compels you to range around the countryside stealing ducks.'

'No, no, *no*, John, you must have mis-heard me on the telephone: duck was not the word I used and it's not me at all, it's some other chap.'

'That's what they all say,' kindly, sadly, 'but tell me all about your, ah, *friend.*'

He was, of course, teasing me, and he knew very well that I knew that he knew that I knew he was, if I make myself clear. I started from the beginning, for I am not skilled in narrative, and went on to the end. It electrified him; he sat up straight and poured profligate drinks for both of us.

'Well, I do call that splendid,' he chortled, rubbing his big, pink hands together. (Can you chortle, by the way? I can giggle and snigger but chortling and chuckling are quite out of my range. It's a dying art, some modern Cecil Sharp should go around recording the last few practitioners.)

'How do you mean, *splendid?*' I asked when the chortling was over. 'My friends and their wives don't think it's a bit splendid, I can tell you.'

'Of course, of course. Forgive me. My heart goes out to them. What I meant was that in the midst of all this bogus satanist revival that's going on it's rather gratifying to a scholar that a serious recrudescence of the real tradition is taking place in just the sort of base and backward community where one had hoped the last embers of the Old Religion might, indeed, still be glowing.' (What lovely sentences he constructs. I wish I could write one half so well as he talks.)

'Yes,' he went on, 'it's all there: the desecration of Easter for a start. It probably starts at Easter every year, you know, but few victims of ravishment ever complain to the police for reasons which doubtless spring to your mind; the counter-accusations and cross-examinations at the trial can be most shaming in cases of this kind. Moreover, the sturdy native Jersey women would, for the most part, appreciate that they had been singled out for what amounts to a religious rite – it is just as if an Englishwoman were told by the Vicar that it was her turn to do the flowers in Church for Easter: a nuisance but an honour. Do you follow me?'

'So far I'm abreast of you.'

'Then there's the inverted cross –'

54

'What inverted cross?' I interrupted.

'Why the one on the witchmaster's belly, to be sure; hadn't you twigged? The ladies would naturally have thought it to be a sword and it may well have been pointed at the top to represent the woven crosses they give out in churches on Palm Sunday, this combining an insult to Christianity and an ancient sex-symbol. Do you happen to know what colour it was?'

'I'm afraid not.'

'Try and find out, there's a dear boy. And find out whether it left any paint marks: it would be quite splendid – that is to say, very interesting – if it proved not to be painted at all but pyschosomatically produced. The body can do wonderful things, as I'm sure you know, under hypnosis or auto-induced hysteria. The stigmata, of course, springs to mind, and levitation: there's far too much evidence to dismiss.'

I shot him a furtive look. He was displaying just a little too much zeal for his hobby-horse; committedness is next to pottiness, especially in elderly dons.

'You are thinking that I am riding my hobby-horse a little hard,' he said – beaming at my guilty start – 'and I confess to finding the subject almost unwholesomely engaging.'

I mumbled a few disclaimers which he waved aside.

'The words "hobby-horse" and "levitation",' he resumed, 'bring us to the next point, the riding-jollop.'

'How's that again?'

'Riding-jollop. There are many names for it but the formulae are all very similar. It is the pungent mixture a witch smears on his or her body before going to the Sabbat. The greasy base stops up the pores and thus subtly alters the body's chemistry, another ingredient reddens and excites the skin, while the bizarre stench – added to the guilty knowledge of what the jollop is made of – heightens the witch's impure excitement to the point where he *knows* that he can fly. In the case of she-witches, a canter round the kitchen with the broom-stick between her legs adds a little extra elation, no doubt.'

'No doubt,' I agreed.

'Whether any of them succeeds in flying is an open question: it is their certain conviction that they *can* that is important. Do you care to know the ingredients of the jollop?'

'No thanks. My dinner sits a little queasily on my stomach as it is.'

'You are probably wise. By the bye, did you happen to notice in your local paper that any new-born babies had been missing shortly before Easter?'

'Whatever has that –?' I said. 'Oh, yes, I see; how very nasty. Do they really? No, I wouldn't have noticed that sort of thing. People shouldn't have babies if they're not prepared to look after them is what *my* old nanny used to say.'

'You might just check, dear boy. It would have been in the dark of the moon before Easter. But of course it might have been the sort of baby which doesn't get recorded. You know, "ditch-delivered of a drab".'

'Just so. "Eye of newt and blood of bat".'

'Precisely. But *try*. Now we come to the toads. I've always felt that Jersey's particular fondness for toads might indicate that it was perhaps the last outpost of the Old Religion, for the toad was easily the most popular Familiar for witches. The warts on its skin, you see, remind one of the extra nipples which every she-witch was supposed to have and that goes back (am I boring you, dear boy? How is your glass?) that goes back to the polymastia or superfluity of breasts of the ancients. I need not remind you of Diana of the Ephesians, who must have looked like a fir-cone, as dear Jim Cabell pointed out.'

'But I thought that the cat was the favourite familiar? I mean, Grimalkin and all that?'

'A wide-spread and pardonable error, Mortdecai. First, you see, by the time of the great witch-hunts of the seventeenth century – best-known because they were politically inspired you see, for there was a sort of suggestion of confrontation between the High Church and Papist Cavaliers, who, oddly, were supposed to more or less tolerate the Old Religion (perhaps they knew how to use it?) and the Puritans, who chose to see witchcraft as an extension of Rome; by this time, I say, the serious witches had gone very thoroughly underground and the only ones left on the surface were a few old crones practising a little Goëtic magic to help their friendly neighbours and to smarten up their petty persecutors.

'Now, the rules of witch-finding were that a witch always had a devil's nipple, by which she could give suck to her Familiar. They used to tie the poor old biddies up and watch them, certain that when the Familiar became hungry it would come around for its rations. Most old ladies, to this day, own a pussy-cat – and most old ladies tend to have a wart or a mole or two, this is common knowledge. You see? Moreover, there is an ancient confusion here, for the word "cat" used also to mean a stick, such as witches might ride on. (Perhaps you played "tip-cat" as a child? No?) In short, you may be sure that the toad, not the cat, is the most popular and effective familiar. "Was" perhaps I should say. Or rather "was deemed to be",' he ended lamely. The warmth of his defence of the toad led me to suspect uneasily that a close search of his quarters would pretty certainly reveal a comfortable vivarium somewhere, bursting with the little batrachians.

'Well, John,' I said heavily, 'that's all quite riveting and I'm more than grateful for the insight you have supplied into the way this awful chap's mind works and so forth, but now I feel we should be thinking about remedies and things, don't you? I mean, to you it's an entrancing piece of living folk-lore, no doubt, but over there in Jersey two of my good friends' wives have been horribly assaulted and one of them, if I'm not mistaken, is in jeopardy of grave mental illness. I mean, conversation of old customs and so on I'm all for, and I'd be the first to join a society for preserving the Piddle-Hinton Cruddy Dance etc., but you wouldn't actually subscribe to a fund for the preservation of the practice of *thuggee*, would you? To my mind, this Johnny should be stopped. Or am I being old-fashioned?'

'Oh Mortdecai, Mortdecai,' he said – how funny it sounded, sort of hyphenated – 'you were always impatient with things of the spirit. I remember you were rusticated in your second year, were you not, for –'

'Yes.'

'And again in your last year for –'

'Yes, John, but is this to the point?'

'Yes, of course, *no*, you're quite right. Remedies are what you must have, I see that, I really do. Now, let me think. We shall assume that the violator is (and I have not a scrap of *doubt* that he is), properly versed in all the side-knowledge of his dread religion. Therefore, he can be daunted in several ways. First and easiest, common salt (rock-salt is better) sprinkled liberally on all entrances into the room; door-sills, window-sills, hearth-stones and even transoms and ventilation-louvres. Second, garlands of wild garlic festooned around those same apertures are reckoned sovereign, but you would be hard put to find wild garlic in Jersey, or anywhere, at this time of the year and its smell is really quite beastly.'

'I know. I have tried to eat wild duck which have been feeding off it. The very dustbin rejects them.'

'Just so. Third, and this has not been known to fail, the person fearful of visitations from a witch or warlock should go to bed clutching a crucifix made either of wood, or, much better, of either or both of the two noble metals – gold and silver: the very best of all is a cross made of one of the hardest woods such as ebony or lignum vitae and inlaid with silver and gold. He or she should memorize a simple cantrip to recite to the emissary of the Desired – chrm – that is to say, the *Evil* One, which I shall now dictate to you.'

'Look John, forgive me, but I don't think we are approaching this on the right lines. For one thing, I've no intention of distributing cantrips and costly crucifixes to every rapable woman in the Parish of St Magloire. For another, we don't want just to keep the beggar out of our bedrooms, we want to catch him if possible – kill him if that becomes necessary – but at all costs to stop him for good.'

'Oh dear, that is a very different matter indeed. You really mustn't kill him if you can help it, you know; he may very well be the last living receptacle of some extremely ancient knowledge, we have no way of guessing whether he has yet initiated a successor to the Black Goatskin. No, no, you must try not to kill him. You might, in any case, find it a little difficult, heh, heh.'

'I know; I'm thinking of ordering a box of silver bullets.'

'My word, Mortdecai,' he cried, clapping his hands merrily, 'you always were a resourceful fellow, even the Dean said as much when you almost won the Newdigate with a thousand lines lifted from Shelley's *Cenci*. Did you get rusticated that time?'

'No, I played the "youthful prank" gambit. The Proctors hit me for fifty pounds. My father paid. I threatened to marry a barmaid if he didn't.'

'There you are again, you see. *Resourceful*. But no, try to avoid killing him. As to capturing him, I really cannot offer any suggestions. He will be endued with Fiendish cunning, you understand, and will have all sorts of other resources which we cannot gauge, it really depends on whether he's been to Chorazin or not.' He seemed to be addressing himself.

'Chorazin?'

'Ah, yes, well, just a scholarly aside, not to the point really. It's a place mentioned in the Bible, just a few mounds today – or so they tell me – and one goes there, or rather chaps like your witchmaster go there, to complete their education, so to speak.'

'A sort of Sabbatical?' I prompted.

'Just so, ha ha. Very good. Yes, they went there to, as it were, pay their respects to Someone; it was called the *Peregrinatio Nigra*, the Black Pilgrimage, you know.'

'Thank you,' I said.

'I'm sorry, dear boy, I had forgotten that undergraduates used once to have a little Latin. Now; catching this chap; I honestly cannot think of a method which would have much hope of success. I suppose one could leave an attractive young woman unguarded in a spinney or copse – but who would volunteer to be the bait? One could hardly *tether* her, could one, it would look suspicious. No, I think your best plan is to fight him on his own terms and bar him from your neighbourhood for good – make him cry *vicisti*, which –'

'Thank you,' I said.

'Oh dear, I'm sorry. Yes; you must give him a whiff of grape-shot and let him know that he's outgunned; he will give you best, I'm sure, and turn his talents elsewhere. In short; you must have a Mass said.'

'A *Mass*?'

'A Satanic Mass, naturally. One of the real, juicy ones. You will then be, as it were, under the protection of his, ah, Supervisor, and he'll have no choice but to leave you and yours alone. You might say it will put the fear of the Devil into him, heh heh.'

I found myself in a quandary. How real was the witchcraft element in our rapist? Dryden, the top scholar in the field, clearly was satisfied that the man was a dangerous adept – but then, how potty was Dryden? Could I go back to Jersey and tell George and Sam that what we needed was a Black Mass? On the other hand, what was on the other hand? Lying out night after night in damp potato fields, hoping that the chap would blunder into one's arms? And what would that prove? Or lie in wait in the wardrobes of likely victims' bedrooms? Quite absurd; moreover, if the Beast of Jersey was any guide, our man would have been watching the chosen house for hours, perhaps days, and rapable women abound in Jersey – if you don't object to legs like bedroom jugs.

'Very well,' I said at length. 'We'll give the Satanic Mass a crack of the whip; I'm sure you know best.'

'Capital, capital; I always said that you were a capable man. I remember saying so to the Dean when –'

'*Yes*, John. Now, how does one go about arranging that sort of beano?'

'Of course, let us be practical. First, we must select a suitable Mass. What? Oh, goodness, yes, there are many. Many. By far the best is the Medici Mass, it never fails, it is positively and finally lethal, but there are no reliable texts of its *Graduale* to be had – all corrupt, every one of them, such a shame. In any case, the *Missa Mediciensis* involves the dismemberment of a beautiful young boy, which I fancy you might think a horrid *waste* – or am I thinking of a chap with a name like yours who came up in the same year as you?'

'Bonfiglioli?' I asked.

'Yes, that was he. Sorry, Mortdecai. And in any case, unless your Jersey witchmaster is uncommonly learned he may not have heard of that particular ritual and it is of the greatest importance that he should *know* what forces you are throwing against him. You see that, don't you?'

'It makes sense, certainly.'

'Ah. Yes. Now I have it: the very one, the *Messe de Saint Sécaire*.'

'And who, pray, was Saint Sécaire?'

'Well, he probably wasn't a saint; in fact he may never have been what you or I would call a *person* even, but his name is known everywhere from the Basque country to the Lowlands-Low amongst the sort of people who know about that sort of thing.'

'You speak in riddles, John.'

'Naturally. Now, you will need only three things: first, an unfrocked priest, for the ritual demands it. I know the very chap: he teaches in a prep-school in Eastbourne and is both reliable and cheap. It will only cost you his steamer-fare – chaps like that never travel by *air* for obvious reasons – and a few bottles of Pastis; some clean straw to sleep-it-off on and perhaps a couple of fivers as a going-away present.'

'I have a servant called Jock who will anticipate his every need.'

'Splendid. Then, you will need a text of the Ritual. There is only one sound copy in existence: it is in the incomparable library of a ridiculous old lecher called Lord Dunromin. I shall give you a letter to him: if you grovel a bit and pretend to believe that he is – as he loves to think – the wickedest man in England, he may be persuaded to let you have a sight of the manuscript and copy out such parts as differ most grossly from the *Ordinale*. Pay particular attention to the peculiarities of the *Introit*, the *Kyrie* and the, well, the *equivalent* of the *Agnus Dei*.'

I scribbled some notes on my shirt-cuff, for I knew that such an anachronism would please him.

'Finally,' he went on, 'and this may be a trifle difficult, you will need a ruined church which has been deconsecrated – preferably one with a toad dwelling beneath the altar. Do you suppose you could manage that, eh?'

'As a matter of fact there is just such a place in Jersey; it's called La Hougue Bie. An abandoned sixteenth-century chapel stands on a mound which contains one of the finest megalithic pre-Christian tombs in Europe. I am sure toads abound there but, should they be absent, it would be the work of a moment – and indeed a kindness – to introduce them to such a haven.'

'Excellent! You are sure that the chapel has been deconsecrated? No? Then you must make sure. You could, of course, *desecrate* it yourself, but it's not really the same thing and you might find the process a little *trying*. There would be, perhaps *annoyances*, in a place of such antiquity. I'm sure you understand me.'

'Only too well.'

'Then I think we have covered everything and you, no doubt, will be eager to get to bed.'

I didn't sleep awfully well, perhaps I'd eaten something which disagreed with me. Once I awoke in a panic: some frightful cantrip had been chanting itself inside my head, but it was only an innocent verse from *The Wind in the Willows*:

'The clever men at Oxford
Know all that there is to be knowed.
But they none of them know one half as much
As intelligent Mr Toad!'

I couldn't understand why it had frightened me so much.

8

By the One who may don the black raiment
Of the Goat which was never a goat
Now come I to exact the dread payment
For the lie that was born in the throat.

In a High Place, to decent men nameless,
Guarding ever the Branchless Rod,
Lies a thing which is pallid and shameless,
Ill with lust for a frightful god.

O, Ashtaroth, darling of Sidon,
Loathly Chemosh, who raves in the night,
I bring the red kiss which shall widen,
For thy servant, a way to thy sight.

Asmodeus

Dryden was kind enough to take me to my train in the morning.
He drives fast and decisively but he has his own little theories about
how to deal with other road-users and the drive was not enjoyable. I
once diffidently pointed out to him that we were entering a one-way
street: he beamed at me, an index finger laid against his nose, and
cried:

'Ah, but *which* way? We are not *told*, you see!' This savouring
of his triumph led him to mount the pavement, so I let the rest
of the trip unwind itself without further comment – and with my

eyes closed. I remember wishing that I knew a cantrip or two to recite.

How Dryden puts you on a train is as follows. He stalls his elderly Wolseley on the 'TAXIS ONLY' sign, leaps out, pops the jack under the sill and gives it a couple of turns. This, he finds, gives him some twenty minutes' grace. Then he strikes a Joan of Arc stance, umbrella pointing to the empyrean, and cries 'Porter!' again and again, in tones of increasing pitch and theatricality, until every sensate being within earshot is frantically seeking porters for the poor gentleman and you, his passenger, are quite magenta-hued with shame and chagrin.

When a porter is at last thrust forward by the compassionate throng, rubbing his red eyes and peering about him in the unaccustomed daylight like a spider evicted from a Scotchman's purse, Dryden takes him firmly by the arm.

'This gentleman,' he explains, laying a forefinger on your waistcoat, 'has to travel to London. It is most important.' He gently turns the porter to the East and points along the up-line. '*London*,' he repeats. 'Pray see to it, and you are to keep this for yourself.' With this he turns away, his duty done, he has *looked after you*. The porter gapes at the tiny coin pressed into his palm, but his sense of humour prevails and he takes your bag with a half-bow and offers to carry your umbrella, too. He leads you to the ticket-office and explains to the clerk just what it is you need. When he has got you into a corner-seat-facing-the-engine in a first-class compartment and has straightened the anti-macassar, he looks around as though seeking a travelling-rug to tuck about your knees. You over-tip him grossly, I need scarcely say. You know that later you may find it all most amusing, but just now you want to spit.

As the train gave a preliminary lurch I rose and looked out of the window. Dryden was on the platform – perhaps he had been asking the guard to *look after* me. But no, he was hurrying along, bobbing up and down to scan first-class compartments.

'Hoy!' I cried, waving. He broke into a canter, but the train was a match for him.

'Turnips!' he seemed to cry as he lost ground. '*Turnips!*'

'Turnips?' I roared, but by then we were out of earshot.

'What the devil does he mean, "turnips"?' I mused aloud as I sat down. Unnoticed by me, the compartment had filled. Opposite me, a respectable old woman, who in the ordinary way would have offered me a religious tract or two, was offering me the nastiest look you can imagine. I played the only possible counter-move: I fished out my silver pocket-flask and took a swig. It did her a power of good. In the diagonally opposite corner sat an albino priest, who looked up from his Breviary to give me a saintly, sloppy smile, as much to say that, if my DTs became intolerable, he would wrestle in prayer with me. The fourth corner was occupied by an obvious merchant-banker – try as they will, they cannot disguise those shifty eyes, that rat-trap mouth. He was working on *The Times* crossword, but to the exclusion of turnips, pocket-flasks and everything else: it is this power of concentration which singles out a man for the merchant-banking trade.

The old lady continued to stare fixedly at the tasteful sepia view of Tewkesbury Abbey, above my head, perhaps willing it to fall on me. I must say I rather liked the cut of her jib, while her clear distaste for the Mortdecais of this world did her credit. I have often thought of acquiring an old lady to keep as a pet. They'd be of little use for a shooting man, of course – no nose, d'you see, and useless over marshy ground – but for the town-dweller they are incomparable. I cannot understand why people pay fortunes for nasty cats and dogs who leave puddles and puppies and kittens all over the place when, for nothing but the cost of her keep, one can have an old lady, clean as a new pin and warranted past child-bearing. Old ladies can help one, too, in countless little ways such as marking shirts and arranging flowers: tricks which few dogs and no cats can be taught. True, they can be noisy, but I imagine that a few cuts of the whip would break them of this – or I dare say they could be surgically muted for a trifling sum. True, too, they are a wasting asset and, if you had the bad luck to pick a poor doer, she might become bed-ridden and linger on for years; a misery to herself and a burden to others. I suppose the thing to do would be to leave, pointedly, a bottle of brandy and a loaded revolver on her commode, as one used to do with a Guards Officer who'd been caught with his fingers in the tambourine.

People shouldn't keep people if they're not prepared to look after them, don't you agree?

London, of course, was hell: it gets worse every day. I pine for the slow, placid, pastoral way of life they still enjoy in New York. Leaving my bag at the Connaught I pottered about until luncheon, having a chat with a shirt-maker here, a haberdasher there and a boot-maker in t'other place. Then I refreshed myself with oysters at a place whose name I shall not tell you, for I do not wish you to go there: you would not like it and there is barely enough room for me.

When it was time to call on Lord Dunromin I made my way to his club, which is one of those ancient, hateful clubs called Bogg's or Crutt's or Frigg's – you know the sort of thing. This particular sink, known to other clubmen as the 'Senior Lechers', is a *bad* place. Members must be old, contemptuous, well-born but spurned by decent society, and expensively dressed in quiet bad taste.

The club porter flicked an eye over my clothes, glanced at the label inside my hat and admitted that the Earl was in the Smoking Room and might well be expecting me. Did I know where the Smoking Room was? I looked at him stonily – I've been squashed by experts. He led me to the Smoking Room.

The Earl didn't get up. He has been the wickedest man in England for years: he now hopes to be the rudest, too. The All-England selectors have long had their corporate eye on him. He looked at my clothes. The two-second glance contrived to embody genuine embarrassment, suppressed amusement and feigned compassion. It was well done; he was in a different league from the hall-porter. I didn't wait to be asked, I sat down.

'How do you do?' I said.

'Oink,' he replied

This brought a waiter. Lord Dunromin loudly ordered 'a glass of the cheese port' for me, while pouring himself something from a decanter at his elbow.

He turned to the window to sneer at a passing omnibus. I studied him. His face was a shade or two darker than my port, a shade or two paler than his. Viewed through my glass, his features became quite black, only the eyes gleaming redly.

'Well,' he said at last, rounding on me, 'are you going to interview me or not?'

This threw me somewhat, but it seemed a small thing to do if it would give him pleasure.

'Of course. Sorry. Now, how long have you considered yourself to be the wickedest man in England?' I asked.

'*Europe*. And I don't like that word "considered". And, since I was fifteen. Sacked from all three Public Schools, both Universities, four clubs and the Foreign Office.'

'My word. And to what do you attribute your success?'

'Lust. What they call sex nowadays. Workin' me wicked will on school matrons, housemaids, chaps' wives, daughters; that sort of thing.'

'Have you enjoyed it all, and have you given it up now?'

'Enjoyed, yes, every minute. And given up now, yes again. Too easy, too tiring, interferes with the television. Watching it, I mean, not the reception, har har.'

I gave him a perfunctory smile.

'Too *easy?*' I asked, as rudely as I could.

'Nowadays, yes, definitely. Look at the way these young fellers with the awful hair get away with it: all pursued by *herds* of young women, lowing with lust, *beggin'* for it. Why, when I was a boy we were proud to get even an ugly bit of crumpet, but look at 'em now – have to fight the gels off. *Pretty* gels, too, ugly ones seem all to have vanished. It's like the policemen, I suppose,' he added cryptically.

'But since those early days, Lord Dunromin, you've never found it difficult, have you?'

'Certainly not. Certainly not. Just the reverse. Indeed, I've never understood why men of our generation' – I started: surely he didn't mean to include *me*? – 'ever found seducin' difficult. I mean, we few really competent seducers can never feel vain about our prowess for we know how absurdly, how *insultingly* simple the whole thing is. I mean, to start with, women are nearly all astonishingly stupid – you must know that – it's hard to believe, sometimes, that they belong to the same *species* as you and me. Do you know that nine out of ten of 'em cannot tell margarine from butter? It's a fact, I promise you, I've seen it proved again and again on the television.

'Then there's another thing in the seducer's favour: almost all women, whether they know it or not, are actually dyin' to be seduced – it's important to them, d'you see. Some want it because they're not married, some because they are; some because they're really too old for it and some because they're too young, heh heh; beautiful women need it to flatter their vanity and ugly ones need reassurance; a very few need it because they're over-sexed but these are the exceptions – most of them are really quite frigid but they go on assuming the horizontal in the hope that their next mount will be Mr Right himself, who will at last waken them and induce in their absurd insides the magical moment they have all read so much about in the garbage they all read. In short, I doubt whether there's such a thing as an unseducible woman in the world. Tragic thing is, not one in a thousand is worth your powder and shot. *Experto crede*. Older ones, by and large, are the best value: they always think it might be their last time, d'you see.'

I'd had quite enough of this, it sounded like an editorial in the *Boy's Own Paper* or an epilogue by a YMCA Warden, but, just as I was about to break in, the Earl was back in his stride, his pink and bulging eyes fixed on the ceiling, his voice sonorous.

'Any man armed with this simple knowledge is invincible: he can cut a great swathe through the female ranks like an Attila as long as his glands hold out. He need not be handsome, glib or rich (although, a motor-car is considered pretty essential these days), indeed, it often rather helps to be poor, scrawny and tongue-tied. Even the portly need not despair, for experienced gels dread the assault of a bony pelvis and many of them associate us chubbier chaps with their fathers, for whom they have usually nurtured a furtive, pubescent passion.

'As I say, the mere knowledge that it's a bowler's wicket should be enough to give the would-be stud all the advantage he needs, but while I'm on the subject I might as well dish out a few practical tips for which I have no further use. Are you taking notes?'

'Well, no,' I said, 'as a matter of fact I –'

'Then do so. Hey, waiter, bring a glass of brandy for my er, for this er, gentleman. No, no, *you* know, that *other* brandy. Now, listen attentively.

'(A),' he said, pronouncing the brackets perfectly, 'you must flatter the target continuously and as grossly as you can without actually giving yourself the giggles – you simply cannot spread the butter on too thick. Never mind if they don't believe it, the subject will nonetheless fascinate them.

'(B); Remember that women *feel the cold*: I cannot stress this too strongly. A woman sitting in a draught is a mere inanimate lump, while a woman with warm hands and feet is an army with its flank turned – a battle half-won. See to it.

'(C); Generations of readers of *Peg's Paper* have been taught that the way to win a man's heart is to encourage him to talk about himself. So *never* talk about yourself at all; this restraint will so craze them with curiosity that they will often surrender their chaste treasure in an effort to win your confidence.

'(D); Fill them to the brim with hot, rich, *food* at frequent intervals, this is both cheaper and better than alcohol, which makes them weep or vomit or behave in other dreary ways. Food induces in them a delicious languor, most conducive to venery. Try some today – you can get it at Fortnum's, of course, and Paxton and Whitfields and, er, Fortnum's . . . places like that.

'(E); Before making the final assault on a woman's virtue, at all costs persuade her to remove her shoes. This can easily be achieved without any appearance of impropriety, yet she will instantly feel pleasantly undressed and vaguely surrendered. (She will also feel *happier*, for her shoes are almost certainly a size too small.) Encourage her to remove the rest of her clothes herself, a little at a time; this puts you in a very strong position indeed.

'(F); Calm her fears continually during the penultimate stage; speak soothing, meaningless words to her as you would to a spirited horse, particularly if she is at all religious. If necessary, you can explain to her that you are not really doing it to her at all: she will believe this against the evidence of her senses if it is put to her reasonably. Indeed, this is sometimes the only way with the very devout ones.

'(G); Take particular care not to ladder stockings, tear shoulder-straps or disarrange hair-styles, particularly if the target is a *poor* gel. Virginities are for giving away, after all, but a good hair-do can cost as much as two or three guineas, did you know that?

'"All this is all very well" I hear you say' – I opened my mouth and then shut it resignedly – ' "and we're damned grateful and so forth, but what about getting rid of them when we've lost interest and have our eyes on a bit of fresh? How about a few tips on that, eh?" "Ah," I reply,' he boomed on, ' "there you have me", for a woman scorned is a pretty adhesive thing and a serious threat to the environment, as they say nowadays. There's no fixed rule. Sometimes you can, so to speak, recycle her by fobbing her off on a less gifted friend but I usually find that the best thing is to be frank and manly about it: explain to the subject in kindly words that she has been but the plaything of an idle hour and that now you propose to cast her aside like a soiled glove. Some will acidly reply that "there's plenty of fresh further up" but most will be so furiously vexed that their love for you will vanish like a rat up a gutter, and they will make their own way to the soiled-glove bin at high speed.'

He chuckled fatly, wheezed, started to cough alarmingly. When he had learned to breathe again I thanked him for his lecturette and reminded him that the subject of my call was yet to be broached.

'How d'you mean?' he snorted. 'Given you enough for a dozen articles.'

'You have indeed, but I'm not a writer, you know, although I may turn to it if I should ever fall on evil times.'

'But you *are* the young feller from the *Gazette* Diary, aren't you?' He was glaring at me with deep suspicion.

'Good God, no!' I cried, shocked for the first time today. 'What a dreadful . . .! I've never been so . . .!'

'Well, who the devil are you, then, and how did you get in here?'

We sorted it out after a while and soon I had wrung from him his slow consent to my having a sight of the abominable Mass.

As I left the Club, I remarked an inky wretch, shaking with alcohol, whining and carneying to the Hall Porter: I wished him joy of his interview.

The Earl's house was but a step away. It was one of those Belgravian massifs with fronts like old Euston Station. The servants in such houses are still English (where do they *find* them?) and the step at the front door is so designed that the butler, when he opens the door, looms over you dauntingly. The one who loomed in answer to my ring was a fine, well-grown specimen who had clearly eaten up every scrap of his gruel when he was a nursling butler. His manner was civil, if condescending, but his eye said that he knew all about gents who wanted to read in the master's library. He stripped me of hat, coat, and umbrella with the ease of a skilled craftsman and led me along a gallery of statuary towards the library. The sculpture was astonishingly fine and of a fruitiness not usually seen outside the rare Supplement to the *Museo Borbonico*. I could not resist pausing in front of an unusually explicit 'Leda and the Swan': I understood at last how the swan had managed the trick. You'd never believe it.

At the end of the gallery there was a sort of vestibule lit only by a concealed ray of light playing on a terminal figure of Pan – the Tree with one Branch – which, as we passed, suddenly became a drinking-fountain in the most dramatic and peculiar way. The butler shunted me into the library, indicated the librarian's desk and left me to my own devices – or solitary vices, as I dare say he thought. I ambled down an alley of shelves crammed with a bewildering accumulation of priceless, richly-bound filth and rubbish. Nerciat rubbed shoulders with D.H. Lawrence, the Large Paper set of de Sade (Illustrated by Austin Osman Spare) jostled an incunable *Hermes Trismegistus*, and ten different editions of *L'Histoire d'O* were piquant bedfellows to De la Bodin's *Démonomanie des Sorciers*.

The Earl's librarian was a pretty slip of a girl with circles under her eyes. She didn't look as though she got much time for reading.

'Are you *Green Girls in Paris*?' she asked. I thought about it.

'No, I'm more the Mass of S. Sécaire, really.'

'Ah, yes. I've put it out for you. It's in a nice plain seventeenth-century cursive without contractions, so you shouldn't have much trouble. I've also put out a plain Latin Missal; it'll save you a lot of time, you need only copy out the variant passages.'

'Thanks, you're very kind.'

'Not at all. That will be fifty pounds, please.'

'Fifty pounds? But surely, that's unheard of between fellow scholars. I mean, common courtesy . . .'

'The Earl is not a scholar and common courtesy is outside his sphere of interest. He has just instructed me on the telephone that the fee is fifty pounds and that you have already had – I think he said racing tips – worth more than that.'

I reflected that George and Sam were sharing out-of-pocket expenses so I coughed up, although with ill grace. She wouldn't accept a Diner's Club card, she wouldn't take a cheque, but she would send a footman round to Carlos Place, where squat the proprietors of my overdraft, buttock-deep in pieces-of-eight. The box-office formalities over, I spent a long and disgusting hour or two copying out the relevant passages of the Mass in a silence broken only by the fidgeting and snickering of the man who had arrived to read *Green Girls in Paris* – an aged person whose thoughts should have been on higher things.

'Faugh,' I thought.

Then I had a bath and a few drinks and things at my own club – a temple of light compared with Dunromin's hell-hole – and flew back to Jersey.

Jock met me at the airport in the 'Big Jam-Jar' as he calls the Rolls. The news was not good. Johanna had not been raped but the wife of a friendly doctor, living a mile from us, had. A bogus call to a road-accident had lured her husband away. The rapist had unscrewed the bulb from the light over the porch and rung the door-bell. The other details were as before.

'And I found out from the new gardener, the old geezer, what this sword on the belly means,' said Jock.

'So have I,' I said. 'Did he seem to connect it with Easter at all?'

'Nah. He kept on saying it was because of the Pakis, which is daft, innit, 'cos there's no Pakis on the Island except them shops in St Helier, where they sell the duty-free watches.'

'Jock, the French word for Easter is *Pâques*: in the toothless mouth of an ancient Jerseyman it would, indeed, sound just like "Pakis".'

'Well, there you are, aren't you?'

'Yes. What's the word on Mrs Sam?'

'Well, not great. I hear she got worse and they took her off to the mainland 'smorning. Mr Davenant's been ringing up to find when you're expected back; he sounds in a bit of a mess.'

'Oh dear, do you think he'll be round this evening?'

'No, he was ringing up from England. He'll be back tomorrow morning, wants to come to lunch.'

'So he shall,' I said. 'So he shall. But, more to the point, is there anything for my supper tonight?'

'Yeah, I got you a nice little treat of kidneys done in wine and mustard on fried bread with a few sauté potatoes all garlicky.'

'The very thing!' I cried. 'I trust you will join me, Jock?'

'Too bloody right I will, Mr Charlie.'

9

What adders came to shed their coats?
What coiled obscene
Small serpents with soft stretching throats
Caressed Faustine?

Faustine

Spring was infesting the air in no uncertain fashion the next day and I awoke, for once, with a feeling of well-being and an urge to go for long country walks. Needing to share this feeling I marched into Johanna's room and flung the curtains wide.

'How can you *lie* there,' I cried, 'with the sun streaming in and all the world going a-Maying?'

I didn't quite catch the two words she mumbled in reply, but they were not 'good morning'.

Soon I was downstairs, stamping about and disrupting the household by demanding a proper breakfast instead of my usual alka-seltzer and dexedrin. It was all quite delicious – porridge and kippers and bacon and eggs and toast and marmalade except that the last mouthful of bacon turned to ashes in my mouth when Jock dumped the mail beside my plate, for on top of the pile lay one of those dread, buff-coloured envelopes marked OHMS. I quaked as I read. Her Majesty's Inspector of Taxes noted with feigned puzzlement that, according to my Tax Return for the previous year, my expenditure had exceeded my income; what, then, he asked with concern, had I been living on? He managed to suggest, although not in so many words, that he was *worried* about me. Was I *eating* properly?

I wrote him a cheque for an entirely irrelevant £111.99 which would fox the computer for a month or two, then I spent a happy ten minutes erasing the name and address on the letter and typing in a fresh one, re-directing it to my new-found friend, the lady-don of Scone College. *Share* the good things of life is what I always say. We shall pass this way but once, you know.

George arrived before Sam and told me about the rapist's latest exploit. He had telephoned the victim's husband that morning for they were friends and had confirmed the gossip that all the nasty magical trappings had been in evidence. There was still no description worth the name: the doctor's wife had tried, sturdy lass, to snatch the man's mask off while he was most deeply preoccupied with his task but he had immediately stunned her with a blow to the temple with the side of his clenched fist – a surprisingly kind blow and, it seemed to me, rather a knowledgeable one. All she could say with certainty was that he was strong, well-built and perhaps in early middle age.

'It seems she's not too shaken up,' George went on, 'been a nurse, you see, in the Army. Hard to shock those lassies. She's more furious than anything else, I gather.'

'And how's Sonia?'

'Oh, well, she still plays up a bit when she remembers to, but on the whole I'd say she was pretty well recovered. Not like poor Vi, she seems to have been knocked for six. By the way, be careful what you say to Sam, he's taking it very hard. Quite murderous.'

Sam entered as though on cue; paler than usual, less kempt, a humourless look on his face. He swallowed half the drink I gave him before sitting down.

'Well?' was what he snapped when he did sit down.

'No, Sam,' I said, 'nothing is well and I should prefer to discuss things after we have all refreshed ourselves a little, don't you agree?' He only glared, not agreeing at all, so I went about on the other tack.

'But first,' I said, 'if you feel like talking about it, we are anxious to know how things are with Violet. Where is she, for instance?'

He finished his drink with a second swallow. It had been really quite a stiff drink for lunch-time. I made him another, giving myself a touch more freedom with the soda-water this time.

'Awful bloody place near Virginia Water,' he said at last. 'Not the big Virginia Water place but one of the other nursing homes round there which specialize in what they like to call Nervous Disorders. Frightful Victorian barracks in Revived Lombardic Gothic; rather like Manchester Town Hall but with rhododendrons and monkey-puzzle trees all around it. Pink, portly consultants flouncing down the corridors, each with comet's tail of adoring matrons and sisters and nurses and lavatory attendants trailing behind them, like little boys following a horse with a shovel and bucket for the good of their father's roses. Foul bitch of a receptionist broke it to me gently that the charges were £60 a day then watched me narrowly to see if I winced. "Payable fortnightly in advance," she went on. I gave her a cheque for eight hundred and forty pounds and she said that "doctor" would probably see Violet that night. I said that for eight hundred and forty pounds "doctor" would bloody well see her there and then. She looked at me as though I'd farted in church. We had *words* then, and I won, although I had to apologize for saying "bloody".'

'I pity the prawn which pits its feeble wits against you,' I quoted. His glare told me that flippancy was not suited to the mood of the moment. (I can't help it you know: some unkind friend once showed me a passage in a Medical Encyclopedia.

'MORIA:' it said – '*A morbid determination to make supposedly witty remarks. Sometimes occurring in people with frontal growths of the brain.*')

' "Doctor",' he went on, 'proved to be a Viennese Jewess –'

'Just like Johanna,' I reminded him brightly, before he could put his foot in it.

'Not at all like Johanna. This was Baudelaire's original "*affreuse juive*", she looked like a malevolent sack of potatoes. But surprisingly civilized and clearly on top of her job. She listened to the receptionist's account of things with her hands folded in her lap, she didn't look at her once but the receptionist was choking back tears in no time. Amazing old bitch. She had that kind of cheerful callousness you only find in the very best doctors: I've no faith in the grave, considerate ones: I knew too many medical students at Oxford. Then she took me up to her office and asked about Violet's people and of course I had to tell her about "Lucia di Lammermoor".'

I made tactful noises. 'Lucia di Lammermoor' is what Sam calls his mother-in-law, who is about as *affreuse* as any mother-in-law can aspire to be. She dresses like a sixteen-year-old in dirndl skirts and little socks, her hair is long and gold and false and her face looks like an accident in a paint-factory. She is always in and out of expensive nursing homes for the nervously afflicted but whether this is just a rich woman's hobby or whether she is a boozer who has to be dried out periodically or whether she really is barmy none of her family has ever decided – or much cared. When last heard-of she had taken wing to North Africa with an eighteen-year-old faith-healer who also happened to be a lift-attendant.

'I gave Dr Wankel – yes, Golda Wankel – the names of the last two loony-bins she's patronized and she rang them up straight away – said it could be important – but neither of them could find the case-history or whatever it's called. Odd, that, don't you think?'

'Only fairly odd.'

'Eh? Oh. I see. Well, then, she asked me all sorts of peculiar things about Violet – does she sort of tend to misinterpret things, does she muddle common turns of phrase – well, you know how we all tease her about saying things like "crafty as a door-nail" and "dead as a wagon-load of monkeys" – and I had to answer "yes" to an awful lot of them, which really made me quite worried.'

His speech was getting a little wobbly: I have a horror of seeing my fellow-men weep. I made him a monstrous drink and tried to change the subject. He took the drink and rallied, but he would not wear the change of subject.

'The next bit was rather awful,' he went on steadily. 'We went up to where Violet had been put – nice enough room – and Dr Wankel squirted some sodium amytal into her. It stopped her staring at one in that awful way but it didn't make her utter at all. La Wankel lifted her arm up (Violet's, I mean) and it just stayed there. Then she bent it and it stayed there, too. She said that's called "*flexibilitas cereas*", which is typical of something or other, it seems. Then she shoved her arms down again and tapped it gently and every time it was tapped it rose a little – like an Anglepoise lamp. That's called "*mitgehen*" apparently. Rather beastly to watch. Then I was chucked out so that Wankel could give her a thorough physical examination and I had to wait outside for about a hundred years. Afterwards I was too knocked-out to pay much attention but I gathered that it was a toss-up whether Violet's trance was depressive or catatonic and that the difference was important. Either way there seems to be a good chance that Violet might suddenly rouse and dive out of the window – the catatonics seem to get the idea that they're angels – and that turns out to mean an agency nurse all round the clock at another huge sum per diem. Then the kindly Wankel gave me a bed – free! – and a pill, and I slept until 'plane-time this morning and that's all.'

I made him another drink, it was easier than saying anything.

Jock, his timing as perfect as ever, announced luncheon and we sat down to gulls' eggs, terrine of rabbit and cold curry puffs. I defy anyone to dwell on private miseries with one of Jock's cold curry puffs melting on his tongue, they stand alone, they really do. We drank bottled beer, for I disapprove of wine at luncheon: it either promotes drowsiness or inflames the animal spirits – either way it wastes the afternoon. Sam was a trifle less jumpy when victualled; George seemed somnolent, unwilling to join in.

'Now,' Sam said, 'tell us about the Oxford venture, Charlie. What did your emeritus Magus suggest?'

I told them, trying to keep the apologetic tone from my voice, doing my best to offer blasphemous folly as the only kind of reason which could prevail. What had seemed to make sense in Oxford sounded merely crack-pot over a Jersey luncheon-table and their blank stares, their shared sidelong glances, did not much help me toward persuasiveness. I ended lamely.

'And if you fellows can offer anything better,' I ended lamely, 'I'd be delighted to hear it.'

There was a long, treacly silence. George ran an exploratory index finger over each hair in his eyebrows, then checked the lobes of his ears and the cleft in his chin before starting to remind himself of the contours of his thumb-shaped nose.

Sam, on the other hand, was motionless, seeming rapt in the study of a curry-stain on the tablecloth.

Jock came in and cleared things away while George and Sam maintained their silences. I was damned if I was going to help them start the ball rolling; indeed, it occurred to me that many worthy people would say that I was damned already.

'All right,' said Sam at last. 'I'm prepared to give it a crack of the whip. If the swine's as demented as he seems to be, then I suppose we can best fight him with this insane garbage.'

George nodded slowly.

'Probably the only language he understands,' he said in a sort of gritty, country-magistrate's voice. 'Distasteful. Probably useless. Certainly expensive. But, as Charlie says, what else comes to mind? Seen stranger things than this taking effect, now I come to think of it. Yes; in India, places like that.'

'You men do realize,' I said, 'that you'll have to sort of participate, don't you? I mean, there's one or two rather dreary things that have to be done during the Mass, you see, and the unfrocked priest will, so to speak, have his hands full for much of the time.'

'Yes,' said Sam.

'Yes, I suppose so,' said George. 'But I'm damned if I'm memorizing any Black Paternosters backwards or any of that rot.'

'Black Paternosters?' I asked. 'Have you been studying the subject a bit, George?'

'We've all read our Dennis Wheatley at some time or another, Charlie,' said Sam.

'Speak for yourself!' I said sharply.

'Let me get it clear in my head,' George said. 'This mummery is supposed to discourage the witch-chap and make him feel that we're as well in with demons and things as he is, so he'd better lay off, is that it?'

'More or less, but there's a bit more to it than that. You see, it embodies a fairly hefty curse which is supposed to make the object of our attentions waste away and die nastily, so if our man really believes in what he's doing and is familiar with this particular ritual – and Dryden is pretty sure he does and is – he ought to be thoroughly scared and might well give up his activities altogether.'

'West African witch-doctors can still do it,' said George. 'Thousands of well-documented cases. If the victim really believes he's going to die on a certain day he just jolly well lies down and dies.'

'Do you mean to say,' Sam asked slowly, 'that there's a chance that this thing might actually kill our man?'

'Well, yes, I'm afraid it seems quite possible.'

'Excellent. When do we start?'

'Just one moment,' said George, 'it's occurred to me – how does the fellow know that this Mass has been performed and what Mass it is and who's on the receiving end and so on?'

'I'm glad you asked that,' I said. 'There's only one way and it will cost us all a certain amount of embarrassment but it will work.'

I then told them the method. After a noisy and acrimonious ten minutes they agreed to it, but our friendship did not come unscathed out of the discussion.

Jock came in at that point with a telegram *on a salver*: he loves to show off in front of what he calls Company. I suspect that he'd really love to be a proper manservant; perhaps I'll buy him a striped waistcoat for Christmas.

The wire was from Dryden. Its wording made me boggle for a moment: 'DESHABILLE ARRIVES FALAISEWISE TOMORROW TURNIP PASTIES ESSENTIAL'.

If Dryden has fault it is that he fancies himself a master of telegraphese; it grieves his friends mightily. There was a time when he could take it or leave it alone but now, I fear, he is 'medically dependent' as the booze-doctors say. The *déshabille* clearly meant 'the unfrocked one', the *Falaise* is one of the Weymouth-to-Jersey mail-packets, 'pasties' was obviously a textual emendation of 'Pastis' by some officious Post Office worker but 'turnip' remained as obscure as it had been on Oxford Station.

'Jock,' I said, 'is there any Pastis in the house?'

'There's a bottle of Pernod, same thing innit?'

'Lay in half a case of Pastis today, please. How are we off for turnips?'

'Funny you should ask that, Mr Charlie; the old geezer in the garden just planted a row 'smorning. Planted another toad, too. But they won't be ready for a couple of munce yet.'

'There should be some of the little French ones in the shops by now. Try the covered market in St Helier, or French Lane. If not, perhaps they can be bought tinned or frozen or dried – I leave it up to you, you understand these back-alleys of the world of retailing – "*nourri dans le sérail, tu en connais les détours*" – but get some by tomorrow night, even if you have to pay cash.'

'Right. How many?'

'How do they sell them, do you know? I mean, by weight, d'you suppose, or by the yard or what? What?'

'By the pound, I reckon.'

'Well, would you say that a couple of pounds would be a good stiff dose for a consenting adult?'

'Plenty.'

'Right, then.'

'Right, Mr Charlie.'

'Fascinating though it is,' said Sam heavily, 'to see you in your rôle of pantry-man, are you certain that there are not subjects of almost equal importance to be discussed?'

I explained all, but neither he nor George was much mollified. Their earlier doubts about our project were renewed by this talk of 'leguminous mystification' (Sam) and 'awful Romish fellows soaked in absinthe' (George). I soothed them a bit but they were still restive. Moreover, they had a scheme of their own up their sleeves which they now insisted we should carry into effect concurrently with the Satanic Mass ploy.

'You see,' said Sam, 'we've been thinking about the victims as distinct from the witchcraft aspect – in case the latter is by any chance a red herring – and, although three victims is not a very useful number to generalize from, one can draw a few tentative conclusions. First, all three families who've suffered are English. This could suggest a hatred for English people generally.'

'It could also suggest,' I put in, 'an *Englishman* who doesn't fancy Jersey women.'

'An *Englishman*?' scoffed George, 'with all that witch nonsense? Tommyrot.'

'I thought we were leaving out the witchcraft aspect for the moment.'

'So we are,' said Sam, 'and your point is well taken, if we are to be logical. But to proceed. George and I are both tolerably well off – though not in the class of the millionaire immigrants who seem so to excite the Jersiais' dislike – but the husband of the last victim, the doctor, is only as rich as a thriving general practice can make him and he has been in Jersey for twenty years, well liked by one and all. However, we are all three in what's called the middle class so it could be a class-hatred or/and an anti-English thing. Notice I say anti-English not anti-British, because Jersey is probably the loyalest of the Crown's appanages. Then there's the age of the victims: they're all in their thirties. This could well be because we all happen to have wives in their thirties or it could indicate that the rapist simply likes women of that age. This could suggest again' – it was choking him to say this, for he was evidently more in the mood for murder than reason – 'that he actually *likes* a good-looking woman in her prime, in what I shall have to call a fairly normal way; I mean, if he was an assaulter of little girls or old ladies we could be sure that he was really vilely mad, couldn't we? The last point is that the three victims are all closely grouped on the map, which suggests a pedestrian, don't you think, or someone who doesn't dare to use a motor-car – unlike the Beast of Jersey, of course, who is supposed to have driven all over the Island to his, ah, targets.'

'Or again, a comparative stranger,' I put in gently, 'like an Englishman who wasn't familiar with all the "back doubles"?'

'Yes,' Sam said patiently, 'it could, indeed, suggest that, too.'

George made that noise, usually rendered as 'Pshaw', which only those who have served in the Indian Army can make.

'So George and I, while you were away, drew up a list, as best we could, of good-looking English women, in their thirties, wives of substantial English *rentiers* or professional men, and living within a mile of here. We believe that the total of probable targets comes to no more than seventeen and that we four (I'm including Jock) could set ambushes which would give us almost a twenty-five per cent chance, each night, of being in the right place.'

'Yes, but how would you convince the rapist, supposing that he is watching the house, that he had a clear field?'

'Easily,' said George, the military man taking over from the back-room boffins, 'so long as we have the cooperation of the, ah, householders.' (One felt that he had almost said 'of the civilian population'.) 'Each of us enters a selected house at the sort of hour when most people are working: say, just before noon – lots of these Jersey workmen spend half the afternoon in pubs, better avoid afternoons. Early in the evening, the husband goes off ostentatiously in his car, loudly saying that he won't be much later than midnight, while wife waves goodbye at door. Then whichever one of us is on guard continues to lie low in the house or, if there's good cover outside commanding all entrances, makes his way to the cover. The wife in question potters about downstairs for a bit then goes upstairs, puts light on in bedroom, perhaps shows herself for a moment at bedroom window, then puts out main bedroom lights, leaving bedside one on, and creeps off to some other room; locks herself in. We lie in wait. Armed.'

'That sounds perfect,' I said cautiously. 'Perfect. Except for a couple of things, if you'll bear with me.'

Sam sighed boredly; George grunted guardedly.

'As follows,' I went on. 'First, just supposing my half-serious theory that it is an Englishman were right, how could one tell that one was not tipping him one's hand and, indeed, guarding his very own homestead?'

'Well, if one must take that seriously, we simply take care not to let any householder under guard on a given evening know which other houses are being guarded.'

'Good,' I said, 'but, better still, let him not know that *any* other houses are under surveillance.'

'Well, all right, that makes sense, come to think of it.'

'Second,' I went on remorselessly, 'what about our wives while we are out boy-scouting? Johanna is a pretty hand with a pistol but even so, without Jock's presence, she might be a bit vulnerable, and she's a natural next target. Sonia may or may not be off the fellow's list now but, after her horrid experience, she probably wouldn't much care to be left alone.'

'Perfectly simple,' George said impatiently, 'Sonia gives a bridge party, invites Johanna, couple of extra men, no one leaves until we return.'

I gaped, horror-stricken. I knew not what to say; I could only shoot a piteous glance at Sam.

'What is uppermost in Charlie's mind, I fancy,' said Sam, 'is that Johanna is really rather in the international league at Bridge – she has partnered Omar Sharif – while Sonia, although she plays with gusto and brio, has this trifling inability to remember what are trumps, and, worse for some reason known only to bridge-players, persists in recanting.'

'Revoking,' I said.

'I dare say you're right, Charlie.'

George assumed his brigadier-voice; just like Matthew Arnold donning his singing-robe.

'Look here, Mortdecai, I'd hate to think that you were making difficulties for the *fun* of it but I must say you're not being exactly constructive in your criticism.'

I cringed a bit; I felt that I had failed the Staff Course at Camberley. Mortdecai would never wear the coveted red tabs on his khaki. 'RTU' (Returned to Unit) would follow his name for ever – never 'psc' (passed staff-college).

'Ah, *shit!*' I thought, as better men have, I'm sure, thought before me, at similar crises in their lives.

'Well,' I said aloud, 'no doubt some other sort of party could be arranged; it's not something to fuss about, is it?'

'That's better.' George was prepared to give the weedy subaltern another chance. 'Of *course* there are other kinds of party: there are whist-drives, are there not, and beetle-drives and canasta-evenings; all sorts of things. One can deal with that sort of detail at, ah, the time.' (Once again, I heard him, almost, say 'at platoon level'. 'After all,' he seemed to be saying 'what are sergeants *for?*')

'Yes, George,' I said, restraining my impulse to call him 'Sir'. 'But my last objection is one that I have raised before. The question of fire-arms. You simple cannot go popping off at people just because they're rapists.'

'I can,' said Sam.

'So can I,' said George.

'Well, I can't. My .455 has to live chained up in the Pistol Club Armoury; my Banker's Special and Johanna's little Savage .28 have to be locked up in bed-side table drawers when we are in and in the safe when we're out. I'd risk *flourishing* a pistol at a miscreant out-of-doors, I suppose, but if I shot someone, except in clear self-defence against an *armed* miscreant, I'd be in line for a long prison sentence. You men would, probably, be in a slightly better position because you've actually suffered from this chap and you'd get the benefit of the "no-jury-would-convict" convention, but I'd look pretty feeble up against a smart barrister explaining that I'd killed a chap because I'd thought he was a chap who'd ravished the wife of a chap I knew, wouldn't I?'

'All right,' said Sam, 'just don't shoot to kill. You're meant to be a first-class pistol-shot, aren't you? Aim at his legs.'

'First-class pistol-shots,' I said, 'know that to hit a human leg in motion with a pistol is a matter of the merest chance. Moreover, the human frame is extraordinarily perverse about dying. You can plant a bullet in the head and the subject walks away – witness that South African premier a few years ago. You can empty a magazine

83

of ammunition into his left breast and he spends a few weeks in hospital, inconvenienced only by saw-edged bed-pans. Yet, pop a small-calibre bullet into the fleshy part of his leg and it nicks the femoral artery and he bleeds to death before the ambulance arrives. You get away with manslaughter and count yourself lucky.'

There was a long and sulky silence. Finally Sam said:

'Argh, go piss up your kilt, Mortdecai.'

'Certainly,' I replied stiffly, 'but I shall require a certain amount of privacy for that. Must you go? Can't you stay?'

'Oh, now, look here chaps,' said George, 'come *on*. Let's not get excited about trifles. It's quite simple and Charlie's talking perfectly good sense. There's no reason why he should risk a prison sentence just to oblige his friends.'

His tone made it clear that *he* would do just that, but that he was a true-born Englishman, unlike certain Mortdecais he could name.

'It's quite simple,' he repeated, 'we all go armed but Charlie carries an empty gun. And a stout stick, or something of that sort. All agreed?'

Sam made the kind of noise you make when you don't mean 'no' but you're too miffed to say 'yes'.

I said, 'Well, now, I'm afraid there's just one more thing.'

'Oh, sweet Christ crucified!' roared Sam. 'What now?'

I didn't take offence this time. He had, after all, been through a bad time. But I had to make the point.

'I'm afraid Jock mustn't carry his pistol at all. His Lüger is highly illegal and moreover he has *form*.'

'?' said George.

'Done some *porridge*,' I explained.

'?'

' "Porridge" is a term used by rats of the underworld,' I said patiently, 'and it means penal servitude. There is a legend, you see, that if, when eating the wholesome breakfast provided on the last morning of your "stretch", you do not eat up all your nice porridge, you will be back in durance vile within the year. Any warder will tell you that. Jock has partly-eaten several plates of such porridge at Her Majesty's expense and if he were to be caught with any kind of firearm at all it would go very hard with him. If he actually shot someone he'd get approximately ninety-nine years: with maximum remission for good behaviour, call it sixty-six. He'd be a hundred and ten when he got out and would expect me to give him his job back, although he'd almost certainly have forgotten how to make decent tea.'

'Oh, stop drivelling, Charlie, your point is taken. Jock will be armed with a stout stick. All right?'

'He has, I believe, a length of lead piping, covered with soft leather.'

'Or a length of lead piping covered with soft leather. Is that all? Then I suggest we start tonight. Here are four sets of names and addresses. Any preferences?'

Quick as a flash I laid claim to Brisbane House, for Lady Quinn-Philpott has the finest cellar in the North of the Island, and no rapist in his senses would tackle her, for her strength is as the strength of ten, because her soul is pure, you see. Moreover, she has a Dobermann Pinscher. The others made their dispositions, leaving Jock, by default, in charge of a tomato-grower's bungalow, inhabited by the most rapable wife you can imagine. Indeed, if Johanna ever left me any time for private study I could quite fancy her myself. I suspected that, if the rapist appeared at that bungalow on that night, he would have to ask Jock to move over.

George telephoned hither and thither arranging for our vigils. Sam seemed to be trying to win a wager as to how rapidly he could empty my whisky decanter. I explained to Jock exactly how my sandwich-case was to be filled. Johanna threw one of her rare tantrums when told that she was to spend the evening playing cards with Sonia. Jock had a shower and overhauled, I daresay, his stock of the products of the London Rubber Company – that excellent condominium. At last they all went away and I was free to do some serious thinking on the sofa, with my shoes off and my eyes closed. A heavy luncheon always brings out the philosopher in me.

The evening's ambuscades were, of course, a complete washout as far as raper-catching was concerned.

I caught an excellent dinner and a splendid bottle of Chateau Léoville Poyferré '61.

Sam caught a strayed Jersey cow in the udders with the unchoked barrel of his shotgun.

George caught a nasty cold from crouching under a hydrangea.

I hate to think what Jock caught but I'm sure it was worth it.

85

When I collected Johanna from the card-party at George's house she wasn't speaking to anyone, least of all to me. I told her about George's ordeal under the dripping hydrangea and all she said was 'lucky George'.

'Good night,' I said as we parted in the hall.

'Good night, Clausewitz,' she replied.

Jock was already abed, sure of a good night's sleep, bless him, so I had to make my own sandwich.

As I stole upstairs with it I felt a sort of strange feeling about Johanna. Had I been twenty – or even fifteen – years younger I would probably have mistaken it for being in love. Perhaps it was a trace of regret for having, so long ago and so rightly, decided that emotion was not for me, that I was better without it. As I hesitated on the landing, the half-gnawed sandwich in my treacherous hand, I had an absurd compulsion to go into her room, to see her honey-coloured hair spread over the pillows and to say soppy, apologetic, *affectionate* things. Make her smile, perhaps. She might have been crying, you see; even women cry sometimes. But I have a fixed rule: whenever you feel like holding someone's hand, have a drink instead – it's better for all concerned in the long run.

I compromised by finishing the sandwich and shuffled off to my lonely bed in a miasma of spring-onions and self-pity: who could ask for more? Borges remarks that there is no more skilful consolation than that we have chosen our own misfortunes. 'Thus,' he explains, 'every negligence is deliberate . . . every humiliation a penitence . . . every death a suicide.'

I brushed my teeth with especial care in case Johanna should take it into her head to come and say good night to me but she didn't of course; they never do.

IO

Thou hast conquered, O pale Galilean; the world has grown gray from thy breath;
We have drunken of things Lethean, and fed on the fullness of death.

Hymn to Proserpine

Kicking and screaming, then whining and sulking, I was wrenched out of bed and sent off to meet the Weymouth packet-boat and Father Tichborne, the practitioner recommended by John Dryden. I call him *Father* Tichborne, unfrocked though he had been, on the same reasoning that my grandmama would have called a '£50 cook', however virginal, 'Mrs' out of courtesy. (Mind you, that was £50 a year *and all found*, which meant four or five gross meals a day washed down with ale and stout; bones-and-dripping money, back-handers from all the tradesmen, the privilege of offering hot mutton sandwiches to Police Constables; the right to persecute everyone below the rank of butler or governess: licence to get hopelessly pissed every six weeks (except in Methodist households of course); at least one kitchen-maid to do all the real work (£50 cooks *never* peeled potatoes) and often as much as seven days holiday a year if you could prove that at least one of your parents was dying. Today, no doubt, they would expect the use of a wireless set, too. You know, those people were *happier* before we started spoiling them.)

Yes, well, there I was on Albert Quay, awaiting the M.V. *Falaise* and Father Tichborne. (*Albert* Quay, imagine! Did you know that both Edward VII and George VI were really called Albert but the

Family wouldn't let them use it on the throne out of reverence for Queen Victoria's Consort and the Privy Council wouldn't, either, because it sounded so common. 'Albert' I mean, not the Privy Council. Both right, of course.) ('This is the last and greatest treason: To do the wrong thing for the right reason' sings Alfred Prufrock, if that's the right way round. And if it matters.)

Yes, well, there on Albert Quay I stood, snuffing the sea breezes until the smell of used beer and vomit and package-tour operators presaged the advent of the *Falaise*.

I spotted him at once, a great rangy buck-priest in a silk soutane. Evil eyes burned from an ascetic face oddly marred by soft and sensual lips, which were just then snarling at the Customs man.

'Hello,' I said, offering a hand, 'my name's Mortdecai.'

He gave me a slow leer, disclosing an assortment of teeth which, had they been cleaner, would have done credit to an alligator.

'And I suppose your friends call you "cheeky",' he retorted, sweeping past me to where a group of saucy-looking lads awaited him. He whispered to them and they all eyed me.

'Isn't he *bold*?' one of them tittered.

Sweating with shame I moved off in quest of the true Fr Tichborne, who proved, when I found him, to be a well-washed, shiny little chap with a face just like that of a Volkswagen. He was sitting on a bench leafing through the latest copy of *Playgirl* with an air of studious detachment and wearing a snappy, dark-green mohair suit which he shouldn't have been able to afford on a prep-school master's salary. Exchanging humdrum civilities, we entered my Mini, where I noticed that he exuded a faint but agreeable smell of seed-cake, which I supposed was really the Pastis escaping from his well-opened pores. As we moved off, he let out a shrill cry of dismay. I clapped the brakes on.

'My corporal!' he squeaked, 'I've forgotten my corporal!' I was alarmed: Johanna is broad-minded about that sort of thing but Jock is not: he would make *remarks*.

'Do you mean,' I asked, 'that you have brought a, er, Non-Commissioned *friend* with you?'

'No no no,' he said testily, 'it's the special *altar* corporal for the Mass we're going to celebrate.'

Mystified, I helped him to search and we found, in the Customs shed, a string shopping-bag containing a lot of folded cloth.

'Do show,' I said.

'Well, not here, I think. The embroidery on it might seem a little, well, surprising, to the casual bystander. And that Customs officer is observing us narrowly.'

On the way home we paused at the 'Carrefour Selous' for refreshment, early though it was.

'This is a very characteristic local inn,' I explained. 'They drink something here called Pastis, I think, and speak highly of it. Would you care to try?'

'I have heard of it,' he said gravely, 'and I long to try it.'

'What do you think?' I asked diffidently a little later.

'Mmm. Quite delicious. Stronger than sherry, I fancy. I say, it won't make me *tight*, will it?'

'I shouldn't think so.'

'But what is that that you are drinking, Mr Mortdecai?'

'It is called whisky. It is a malt liquor distilled in the highlands of Scotland. I believe they sell quite a lot of it in Jersey.'

We gazed at each other with straight faces. He was the first to laugh – after that there was no embarrassment. It takes one to know one, they say; whatever that means.

Johanna took to him on sight, which was reassuring for she is never wrong about people, whilst I almost always am. She was fussing over him and telling him how tired he must be and what could she offer him to drink (ha ha) when Jock loomed in the doorway and announced luncheon in the doom-laden voice of a servant who is in the mood to give in his notice at the drop of a hat.

'This is Fr Tichborne, Jock,' I said brightly.

'Reelly,' he said.

'Yes. His bags are in the car – perhaps you would bring them in presently.'

Jock turned on his heel and clumped towards the door.

'Oh, and you could bring his corporal in, too?'

Jock ground to a halt and looked over his shoulder in a dangerous sort of way.

' 'Is *wot?*'

'It's in a string bag,' I explained blandly. It made my day, it really did, although I knew I'd pay for it.

Johanna insisted on seeing the corporal and although Tichborne blushed and demurred she got her way. She usually does.

'You see,' said Tichborne anxiously as he unrolled the cloth, 'one can't use the consecrated corporal – for one thing it might put off the sort of person we're hoping to, er, invoke, and for another it would be *rude*, simply; I mean, I always believe in extending common courtesy to what I might call the Other Side, even though one has to be a bit horrid about Them during the actual ceremony. Do you follow me?'

We made guarded noises.

'Moreover, this sort of Mass used to be performed on the, er, person of a young *person*, so to speak, but we've found that using a corporal depicting such a young person in the appropriate attitude serves just as well. I mean, I do speak from some experience.'

The cloth was now unfurled and spread out on the sofa-table. I must say that even I found it a little startling: the appropriate attitude of the young person certainly seemed to speak from experience, to use Tichborne's phrase, and the embroidress had been explicit to the last prick of her needle, if I may coin another. Both Tichborne and I cast worried glances at the gently-nurtured Johanna.

'Wow!' she exclaimed politely, 'that is really out of sight!' (She only uses Americanisms defensively.) For my part, I wished heartily that the thing *were* out of sight, lest Jock should come in. (Most brutal criminals are *prudes*, did you know? Of course you did, forgive me.)

'You can say that again, sister,' I growled, falling into her vernacular. She looked at me strangely, perhaps admiring my gift of tongues.

'You mean the "Wow",' she asked, 'or the other bit?'

'Never mind.'

'But this lovely needlework must have cost a fortune, Father Tichborne,' she resumed, 'wherever did you get it made?'

'As a matter of fact I did it myself,' he said, crimson with shame and vanity. 'It took ages, I don't mind telling you.'

'Working from life, evidently?' I put in.

'Well, no, more from memory, really.'

It seemed a good point at which to end that conversation. As we rolled the corporal up George arrived to inspect Fr Tichborne.

Introduced, he made the civilizedest noises he could muster, giving the impression that, in his view, the only good Papist was an unfrocked Papist.

Tichborne gained a little ground by asking him about his regiment but lost it all again by saying that he himself had been a chaplain with the Free French.

'I'll just bet you were,' said Johanna brightly.

George's face turned a sort of pale shade of black; he took it rather hard.

'The French were on our side, George,' I reminded him. 'This last time, I mean.'

'You will stay to lunch, won't you, George?' said Johanna.

He couldn't, he had another appointment, he'd already had luncheon, he never ate luncheon, Sonia was expecting him for luncheon, he had a train to catch. There are no trains on Jersey, of course: I think he just wanted to go and kick something. It's all to do with a place called Dakar, for some reason.

Luncheon was rather awful at first: it was the cook's day off and therefore Jock had the duty and you could see that he didn't much relish waiting on Fr Tichborne. He served soup to Johanna, then, despite my coughs and glares, to me. I gave Tichborne an apologetic grimace. His plate of soup arrived quite three minutes later.

'Dash it, Jock,' I snapped, 'your thumb is in Fr Tichborne's soup!'

' 'S all right, Mr Charlie, it ain't hot.' Tichborne frowned at me and shook his head, so I let it pass.

The next thing was kidneys wrapped in bacon and stuffed into baked potatoes. Quite delicious, except for Tichborne's, which was small, late and badly burned.

Really angry now, I opened my mouth to admonish Jock severely, but Tichborne raised his hand.

'Jock,' he said in a quiet, gentle voice, 'once is happen-stance, twice is coincidence, three times is enemy action. By that I mean that if you once more disgrace Mrs Mortdecai in this shabby way I shall take you out into the garden and punch your nose quite flat.'

An awful silence fell. Johanna's eyes were wide open, as was my mouth. Jock started to swell like a bull-frog. Fr Tichborne poured himself a glass of water.

'Gaw blimey!' said Jock at last.

'Guard your tongue!' commanded the little priest in a voice of thunder. 'The words you have just uttered mean "God blind me" – you have already lost the sight of one eye: be very careful Whom you invoke to pluck out its fellow.'

I glanced up: no plaster was falling from the ceiling.

The awful silence went on.

Finally Jock nodded and vanished into the kitchen. He emerged and laid a large and beautiful kidney in front of Fr Tichborne.

'You better have mine,' he said. 'Sir.'

When the green baize door had closed behind him, Johanna said, 'Golly.'

Fr Tichborne said, 'I believe I've made a friend.'

I said, 'You must come and stay *often*.'

Later, as we mumbled a little cheese – Brie, I think it was – mounted (the cheese, not us, of course – I *must* learn to be lucid) – the cheese, I say, mounted on Mr Carr's incomparable Table Water Biscuits – goodness, what a muddle this sentence is in, as dear Judge Jeffreys said at the Bloody Assize; let me start again. During the cheese-eating period I apologized to Fr Tichborne that I had not been able to offer him any turnips with his luncheon but that I was having the market scoured and hoped to be able to make those sapid roots manifest at dinner.

'Turnips?' he said, faintly. '*Turnips*? This is uncommonly thoughtful of you but, to be frank, it would be disingenuous of me to pretend that I was a *leading* turnip-eater.'

'Not?' I said puzzledly. 'But Dr Dryden assured me, albeit cryptically, that turnips were of the very essence.'

He cogitated puzzledly awhile.

'Hah!' he cried at last. 'Hah! Of course!'

'Yes, yes,' we agreed, 'of course . . .?'

'No no,' he went on, 'I see, I see; he knew I would need a slice or two of turnip for our ritual. You see, at the, ah, *equivalent* of the Elevation of the Host one must either use a consecrated Wafer which has been desecrated – and I've told you how I hate to be rude to the Other Side – or one must bake a travesty of it oneself (naughty old Sir Francis Dashwood and his Hell-fire Club chums used to call it a "Holy Ghost Pye") or, best of all, one uses what one might call a caricature of the Host: in fact, one makes it out of a slice of turnip. Stained black, you know, and cut into, well, a sort of curious shape, if you follow me.' He looked at us worriedly. 'It gives less offence, you see,' he went on, 'and it seems to work quite as well. *Quite* as well. Really.'

'Would you like some coffee?' said Johanna.

That afternoon, all friends now and all full of luncheon – for I fancy Jock had scoffed a moody tin of caviare – we set off for a reconnaissance of the chapels, furnished with a capable picnic hamper in case the sun shone.

I'm sorry, but I shall have to explain about these chapels. There is a place in Grouville Parish, in the East of the Island, called La Hougue Bie. I believe no one is certain what the name means. It is a monstrous, man-made mound inside which, only excavated fifty years ago, there is a dolmen: a tomb made some five thousand years ago of great slabs of stone. To reach the main tomb-chamber you have to creep, bent double, for what seems a very long way indeed along a stone tunnel. If you are claustrophobic, or superstitious or simply a coward, then you will find it a dismal and grimly place indeed. I hate it for all three reasons and I hate, too, the thought of the brutish folk who built it; I loathe to speculate on what disgusting compulsion made them drag and raise those monstrous stones and then spade over them those countless tons of earth, all to encyst some frightful little prehistoric Hitler.

Nevertheless, I believe that we should all visit such a place from time to time, in order to remind ourselves how recently we sprang from the brutes.

Crowning the great mound and, curiously, exactly above the main tomb-chamber, someone in the twelfth century raised a decent little chapel dedicated to *Notre Dame de la Clarté*. A few centuries later another decent chap dug himself out a crypt in the pious – if mistaken – belief that it was a replica of the Holy Sepulchre itself, and then tacked another chapel onto the first. This latter is called the Jerusalem Chapel.

I didn't go into the dolmen myself; once had been enough for me – I just don't enjoy feeling my flesh crawl. Jock was prowling about the surrounding area looking absurdly like a professional crook but the nice tourists paid him no heed: they probably assumed he was a security-firm guard, there's no telling the two apart, is there? Fr Tichborne, on the other hand, dived into the dank darkness of the tunnel with every sign of relish and emerged looking flushed and excited, like a young bishop with his first actress.

'Do you have a portable tape-recorder?' were his first words.

'Of course I have, who hasn't? But whatever for?'

'Tell you tonight. After dinner.' And with that he dived back into the hell-hole. I spent five instructive minutes in the excellent little Agricultural Museum near the mound, marvelling at the monstrous tools the tillers toiled with in the olden days. How they must have sweated, to be sure; it made me feel quite faint.

When Tichborne re-emerged we rounded up Jock and 'cased' the chapels. ('Cased', you understand, is a piece of thieves' cant meaning 'surveyed with intent to commit a felony' – but I dare say that you, who must be the sort of person who reads this sort of story, would know that sort of thing already.)

The earlier chapel – *Notre Dame de la Clarté* – exhibited a notice saying that it had been 'recoiled' by some meddlesome bishop with too much time on his hands. Tichborne explained that this meant sort of re-consecrated and de-Romanized.

'Drat it,' he added petulantly.

The Jerusalem Chapel, however, displayed no such advertising matter and Tichborne said that it would do beautifully – almost certainly disused since they closed all the chantry-chapels after the Reformation thing in 1548, he told us.

'Reelly?' said Jock.

In the car going home we asked Jock whether it would be practicable to gain access to the chapel and dolmen by night in a clandestine fashion.

'A doddle,' he replied. 'Just a doddle. The gate into the grounds isn't worth opening, you can nip over it easy if your piles are better this week. Sorry, sir.' (I was startled until I realized that 'sir' was meant for Tichborne – then I was a little *piqued*.) 'That underground tomb,' he went on, 'has got a first-class padlock but the chain to it is no better than the common shit-house variety (beg pardon, sir) and a liddle old pair of wire-cutters will soon sort that out.'

'Ah,' said Tichborne, 'but what about that formidable great iron lock to the chapel?'

Jock made a coarse noise by expelling air from between his closed lips.

'That ain't a formigal lock,' he said contemptuously, ' 't'ain't even a Yale; it's just *big*. I could open that bugger with me old . . . er, I could open that lock with any old bit of wire. No sweat.'

'Jock,' I said, 'pray stop the car at the next decent inn or hostelry so that I may buy you a large and toothsome drink. "Thou shalt not muzzle the ox when he stampeth out the corn" is what I say. So did Deuteronomy.'

'XXV; 4,' agreed Tichborne.

'Reelly,' said Jock.

That night, after dinner (I think it was *Médaillons de Chevreuil S. Hubert au Purée de Marrons* with a saucy little Chambertin on the side, unless it was a Friday, in which case Jock would have gone out to fetch fish and chips) that night, I say, I reminded Fr Tichborne about his interest in portable tape-recorders.

'You were going to explain about portable tape-recorders,' is how I put it to him.

'Yes, yes,' he said, 'I believe I was. Yes, so I was.'

His childlike eyes flitted about wildly as he sipped at Johanna's incomparable, inherited brandy: one got the impression that it was not quite his *bag*, as the children say nowadays.

'I must apologize for this brandy,' I said, flicking a glance at Johanna. 'For my part I believe I'd rather have some of that Pastis stuff: could you face it? I daresay there's some in the house . . .?'

A few gollups of Pastis later (it's really just absinthe without the wormwood) he was relaxed and expansive.

'Do you promise not to laugh?' were his first words.

We crossed our hearts.

'Well, two years ago I read a book by a man called Konstantin Raudive. It's a perfectly respectable book and endorsed by respectable scientists. Raudive claims, indeed proves, that he heard gentle chattering and muttering coming from the unused intervals of tape from his recorder. I had had the same experience but had put it down to the random wireless reception . . . er, *radio?*'

'Wireless is fine with me,' I said.

'Oh, good. Well, as I say, I had thought it was the sort of stray reception that people get from hearing-aids and things but after

95

reading Raudive I naturally tested it and found that even on virgin tape I still got the gentle muttering if it was played through on "record" in silence and at a nil recording level. Like Raudive, I found that if I boosted the gain when playing-back it sounded uncommonly like speech, but with quite strange intonations, odd grammatical sequences, random relevance.'

Johanna rose, excused herself gracefully and said that she really had to go to bed. She hates long words, although she is very clever. (Why do I persist in entangling myself with clever women when the only ones I find truly adorable are the transcendentally stupid, the ones whose intellects are bounded on the North by the ability to count to nine? Alas, the latter get rarer every day. '*Il y a des gens qui rougissent d'avoir aimé une femme, le jour qu'ils aperçoivent qu'elle est bête. Ceux-la sont des aliborons vaniteux, faits pour brouter les chardons les plus impurs de la création, ou les faveurs d'un bas-bleu. La bêtise est souvent l'ornement de la beauté; c'est elle qui donne aux yeux cette limpidité morne des étangs noirâtres et ce calme huileux des mers tropicales.*' I forget who wrote that. Probably not Simone Weil.)

'Do go on, Fr Tichborne,' I said when the good nights were over.

'I say, would you care to drop the "Fr" now?' he asked. 'The boys at school call me "Eric" – I can't imagine why, for it's not my name, but I quite like it.'

'Please go on, Eric. And pray call me "Charlie".'

'Thank you. Well, once I got the hang of these odd attempts at communication, I found them quite, well . . .'

'Mm?'

'Interesting,' he said defiantly. 'Interesting!'

Trying, as ever, like Caesar's wife, to be all things to all men, I tried to help.

'But disturbing?' I guessed.

'Yes, that too. Certainly that. Disturbing is a *good* word. You see, I began to recognize voices and to unscramble them and they were all from dead chaps, you see, like my old headmaster and the Principal of my Seminary and people whose books I had read – well, of course I couldn't recognize their voices but if you hear a chap talking really barbarous Latin with a strong Slav accent and telling you not to wash because it's a sin of fleshly luxury and then he says his name is Jerome, what can you think?'

'What indeed?'

'Quite. But I felt that I had to go on taping and listening and trying to hear and understand and it got worse.'

I slid some more Pastis into his glass, added a little water and helped him aim it at his mouth. He wasn't drunk, I think he was in some sort of private ecstasy, like a menopausal woman thinking about Cassius Clay.

'It got worse?' I prompted.

'Much worse. Cardinal Manning shouted and *shouted* at me and seemed to know all about my, er, case; and then someone calling himself Pio Nono kept on saying that he would pray for me but that he couldn't promise anything and then, worst of all . . .' His voice broke.

'Your mother?' I asked gently.

'Oh, no, she's always very understanding. It was St Francis. At first I hoped it was Francis of Assisi but he soon put me right: it was St Francis *Xavier*. He was horrid to me. Horrid. You can have no idea what that old bastard can be like.'

His eyes were full of tears. Well, of course, I know what to do with drunken nut-cases. You humour them, listen to them, get them really pissed, then put them to bed, first loosening their collars and removing their boots. My only pre-occupation was how to loosen a Roman collar and how to prevent Eric from moistening my landlord's rather good Empire sofa.

'Look,' he said suddenly and articulating clearly, 'would you like to hear? Please?'

'Certainly, certainly; I'll go and fetch the tape-recorder. Tell you what, let me just freshen up your glass first.'

I fetched my rather good tape-recorder, broke open a new sixty-minute blank tape, fed it deftly into the machine and set it ready for action at $3\frac{3}{4}''$ per second. Eric gazed at the machine in an ambivalent sort of way, as you or I might gaze at the dentist's drill, which both giveth and taketh away pain. He went on gazing until I sort of shuffled and fidgeted. He looked up at me with a startling, seraphic smile.

'Forgive me,' he said, 'I should have told you. All these phenomena seem to be linked to an alpha-rhythm in the brain of around eight to twelve cycles. It seems that people who can do telepathy and telekinesis and thing like that are people who can more or less organize their alpha-waves. Sometimes it can be induced by hypnosis, sometimes it just occurs naturally when one is falling asleep or in a half-aware condition when awakened from sleep too soon; adolescents and menopausal women can often induce it by thinking unclean thoughts with their eyes shut. Mediums who insist on half-darkness and silence and so forth during their parlour-séances are usually, if they're at all genuine, fumbling for conditions in which they can depress their alpha-waves to the required level, whether they know it or not. I suspect that many "fake" mediums are women who are genuinely receptive at times but do not understand how to set up the conditions properly and so fudge the results when it doesn't really work.'

I was a little taken aback. Not much of this made a great deal of sense to me, but it certainly didn't sound like the ramblings of a drunkard.

'They've done a lot of work on this in the Soviet Union,' he went on, 'and I must say that it does rather look as though their approach has been rather more intelligent than the Americans. I mean, they feel that things which are clearly outside the laws of science as at present understood cannot be examined by standard scientific methodology. Like trying to weigh neutrons on a grocer's scales, do you see.'

'That seems reasonable to me,' I said. 'I remember saying to one of those psychic/psychologic researchers from a comic new University – Lancaster? – that most poker-players are familiar with that rare and wonderful feeling which occurs perhaps once in a thousand hands, when they *know* they cannot lose: I told him that I'd had it twice and so strongly that I hadn't looked at my hand, hadn't drawn to it, had betted it to the hilt and had not been in the least surprised when I'd won. The researcher-twit's reaction was to deal me singles from a cold pack of cards, inviting me to guess the colours. My results were nine per cent below random probability, or whatever they call it. That made me a liar in his eyes and him an idiot in mine. I could have told him, had he had the wit to ask, that the necessary conditions were that we should have been playing a real game for several hours, that I should have ingested perhaps a third of a bottle of brandy, that I should have been slightly ahead of my table-stakes by virtue of the ordinary run of cards and that, in short, I should have been in that state of drowsy euphoria where I was effectively asleep in all bodily departments except my card-sense.'

'You couldn't have put it better!' cried Eric. 'All the conditions were there, you see: mild fatigue, mild euphoria, mild depression from the brandy – I'll bet your alpha-waves were at something very like ten cycles per second.'

'No takers,' I said.

'Quite. By the way, I'm sorry to say "quite" all the time but much of my work lies amongst Americans and they *expect* Englishmen to say it.'

'Just so,' I said.

'Whether these receptions, if that is a useful word, come because of me, or through me, or merely *from* me, I cannot say,' he went on. 'So far, however, like Raudive, I must admit that I have not encountered any words which were in a language I did not know, nor from any sources with which I was not familiar. This might seem to suggest that I am, as it were, the prime mover; but it could just be a communication-problem, don't you think?'

I didn't mean to say 'quite' but it seemed to slip out. I poured him some more Pastis and gave him a friendly grin, which probably looked more like a rictus.

'Well,' I boomed uncertainly, 'let's have a shot, shall we?' He did his gazing act again for a minute or two, then put an arm protectively around the machine and sort of nestled against it as he switched on. He gazed moonily at the revolving tape for five long minutes, then shook his head violently and rewound the tape to the beginning.

'No good?' I asked cheerfully.

'Can't say.' He turned the gain up to about half-strength and pressed the 'play' key. The machine began to emit the usual 'white noise' and machine noises and the gentle susurrus of his breathing; nothing else. I was embarrassed for him, wished he hadn't started this nonsense, wondered how I could help him talk his way out of the let-down.

'D'you hear it?' he asked suddenly.

'Oh, Christ, he really is barmy,' I thought, making an apologetic grimace at him, as one does to chaps who point out pink elephants in the corners of a room. He turned up the gain – and I heard it. A

99

soft, infinitely distant twittering, then a chuckle and a protracted cackle which rose and fell in an oddly odious way.

He tinkered with the volume and speed-controls here and there and played with the 'cue' and 'review' keys until suddenly, rising clear and sweet over a tangle of gibberish, a laughing voice quite clearly said:

'FILTH! Filthy sot! Filthy sot? Filthyfilthy filthyfilthy *filthy-filthy*,' on a rising scale which ended with a bat-like shrill which hurt the ears. Eric pressed the 'pause' key and looked at me, his eyes brimming with happy tears.

'That's my mummy,' he said. 'She worries about me a lot.'

There was a time when a remark like that would have given me no trouble: I would have tossed off a rejoinder both witty and respectful, but I am no longer the man I once was. All I could find to say was, 'Really?'

'Oh, yes,' he said, 'she usually comes on before the others start and says something playful.'

'Others?'

'Oh, lots of others. Let's try.'

He fiddled with the knobs and things again and, in a little while, isolated a hoarse, gin-soaked voice, choking with passion, which said *'De profundis clamavt ad te, Domine'* again and again in tones of bitter reproach.

'Not anyone from antiquity,' said Eric. 'That's the sort of Latin that Irish priests still learn in their seminaries today. The speed's not quite right; he sounds lighter than that if one can hit the exact speed.'

'Oscar Wilde on his death-bed?' I couldn't help asking.

'Do you know, you might be right, I really think you might.'

We did not have much more luck, if that's a suitable word, from then on. Someone did some peculiarly unpleasant laughing, Eric's mother came through again in a flurry of animal noises and seemed to accuse him of having practised something which would have brought a blush to the hairy cheeks of old Krafft-Ebing himself ('She will have her little joke,' Eric murmured uneasily) and, near the end, a still, small voice delivered a message plainly intended for me, concerning a matter which Eric could not possibly have known about, and with which I do not propose to trouble the reader at this point. Or ever.

Oh, yes, and whenever we hit one particular speed/volume combination an urbane and friendly voice repeatedly said, 'No, don't. Don't. Not tomorrow. No, I really wouldn't. Not tomorrow. Don't, please.'

'All quite fascinating,' I said heavily when Eric had at last switched everything off. 'Fascinating. It seems to me, though, that it might not be a good idea to let every Tom, Dick and Harry share this sort of, ah, recondite harmony, perhaps?'

'Goodness, no. I only do it when I'm alone or with people of quite exceptional emotional stability – like yourself, if I may say so.'

I didn't – couldn't – comment on this astonishing assessment of me: I keep my emotional stability and things like that at the bottom of my handkerchief drawer, along with the vibrator and the naughty photographs, as W.H. Auden has probably already said. It was the other part of what he said that drew my fire.

'Do you mean to say that you sometimes do this sort of thing *alone*?' I asked, wonderingly. 'At *night*?'

'Goodness, yes. Often. What have I to be afraid of?'

I didn't answer that. If he, with his qualifications, didn't know, it wasn't my place to tell him. I mean, I wasn't his bloody *Bishop*, was I?

He was smart enough, however, to notice that I was becoming moody and he set himself to the task of amusing me, with some success. I yield to few when it comes to telling dirty jokes but it takes a seminary priest to tell a true Catholic story with the right admixture of shyness and authority. He had this art to such a state of perfection that I recall falling about a good deal.

Later, he taught me how to make and drink a 'nose-dive' – an art little known outside the campus of the University of Southern California, where Eric had once spent a happy semester teaching the well-nourished undergraduate girls there the full inwardness of Verlaine's *Chansons Pour Elle*.

How you drink a 'nose-dive' is as follows – you ought to know because it is the only way of gagging down the nastier forms of alcohol, like tequila, pulque, Polish vodka at 149° of proof, paraldehyde and aircraft de-icing fluid. You fill the shot-glass with the desired but normally undrinkable fluid and place the shot-glass inside a high-ball glass, which you then fill, to the level of the shot-glass, with iced orange-juice or some other sharply nourishing

101

fluid. Then you drink it all down as one. The juice, unpolluted with whatever lunatic-soup happens to be in the shot-glass, nevertheless marks its horrors during the progress over your palate. As a bonus, at the end, the adhesion of the inner glass fails and it slides down and bumps you gently on the nose – hence the name of the game. The nose-bumping, I may say, in my experience compels you irresistibly to repeat the process. I have no knowledge of other mixtures but I don't mind telling you that, practised with Pastis and pineapple-juice, you soon find yourself sitting on the carpet, singing songs you didn't think you knew the words of.

It seems to me, but I cannot be sure, that Jock entered the room in the small hours and, with many a kindly word, showed Eric where his room was; returning later to take me out to the shrubbery and hold my head, then to the shower-bath. And so, I dare say, to bed.

Anyone will tell you that there's nothing like Pastis to take one's mind off the things tape-recorders say to you.

II

Now all strange hours and all strange loves are over,
Dreams and desires and sombre songs and sweet,
Hast thou found place at the great knees and feet
Of some pale Titan-woman like a lover,
Such as thy vision here solicited,
Under the shadow of her fair vast head,
The deep division of prodigious breasts,
The solemn slope of mighty limbs asleep,
The weight of awful tresses that still keep
The savour and shade of old-world pine-forests
Where the wet hill-winds weep?

Ave Atque Vale

For years I had believed that these lines:

'Shot? So quick, so clean an ending?
Oh that was right, lad, that was brave;
Yours was not an ill for mending,
'Twas best to take it to the grave'

were about a horrified young Edwardian who had discovered that
he was a homosexual. I am in a position to correct literary history
in this matter. The lines are about a horrified chap in early middle
age who has discovered, one morning, that he has no head for Pastis.
This, you see, was not the common hangover of commerce, it was

a Plague of Egypt with a top-dressing of the Black Death. Quite clearly incurable. I touched the bell.

'Jock,' I said hollowly, 'pray bring me a pot of tea – the Lapsang Souchong Tips I think – and a loaded revolver. Mine is not an ill for mending: I propose to take it to the grave but I wish to blow the top of my head off first. I have no intention of spending eternity with the top of my head in its present condition.'

He started to steal away.

'Oh, and Jock,' I added, 'when you bring the tea-tray I implore you not to let the spoon or other cutlery rattle against the revolver.'

'Yes, Mr Charlie.' Was there a tinge of contempt in his voice?

I lay there listening to the surly, ragged beating of my heart, the tidal noises my liver was emitting and the figured-bass in the back of my skull. A silvery laugh floated up to me from the kitchen: how could Johanna be *laughing* at a time like this – she should have been on her knees beside my bed, promising to hold my memory sacred forever.

A few feet from where I lay there was a window: a small, diligent spider was spinning a web in one of its corners. He was spinning it *inside* the double-glazing, I have never seen anything more piteous in my life, it made me think of me. I dare say I shed a tear or two. Had a capable Jesuit entered at that moment he could have bagged my soul without firing a shot.

What in fact entered was my tea, borne by Jock with a minimum of clamour. I had some difficulty getting into a position where I could sip it; my bottom kept on sliding down the silk sheets. (How I have longed to have been born of common stock so that I could sleep on kindly Irish linen, but, alas, rank has its obligations as well as its privileges.)

I shall not say that the first sips revived me, for I have ever loved the truth, but it is a fact that they allowed me to contemplate the bare possibility of continuing awhile in this vale of tears.

'Jock,' I said sternly, 'I can distinctly hear Mrs Mortdecai laughing. Explain this as best you can.'

'Couldn't say, Mr Charlie. She's having breakfast with Farver Tichborne and they seem to be relishing it no end.'

'Breakfast!' I squeaked. 'Breakfast? Tichborne is eating *breakfast*?'

'Too right he is. He's had a plate of porridge with cream and sugar, then another plate Scotch-style with salt and dripping and pepper, then two eggs boiled very soft and runny, with richly-buttered toast, and now they're starting on a pound of devilled kidneys with smoked salty bacon. I better run down and see if they'd fancy a bloater or two, I got some lovely ripe ones in the market yesterday.'

'Get out,' I said.

'You fancy anythink?' he asked.

'*Out!*' I cried.

'You ought to try and get something down you, Mr Charlie, you look a bit rotten. Eyes like piss-holes in snow, if you'll pardon the expression.'

I turned my face to the wall, feeling like a collection of passages deleted from the Book of Job.

Even the Job's comforters were not wanting, for, half an hour later, some traitor downstairs allowed my kindly extrovert landlord to invade my death-chamber.

'Hullo hullo hullo!' he boomed. 'What, still slugging abed? You're missing the best part of the day!'

'I'm poorly,' I muttered.

'Rubbish!' he bellowed. 'Nothing a breath of fresh air wouldn't drive away in a trice. It's a *splendid* morning!'

Now, the first thing to remember about landlords is that you cannot tell them to fuck off.

'It's raining,' I said sullenly.

'Certainly not. Not a bit. A fine, brisk morning; clear and cold. Not a spot of rain.'

'It is raining in my heart,' I said coldly. '*Il pleut dans mon coeur comme il pleut sur la ville.*'

'Ah, well, yes, I daresay, but mark my words . . . '

'When you go down,' I said, 'would you be kind enough to ask someone to bring me up a basin to be sick in?'

'Right, well, that's me, I'm off; lots to do. Look after yourself, won't you.'

'Thank you,' I said.

There was nothing for it but to get up, so up was what I got. My symptoms started to sagashuate again but Jock blocked my every move to slink back into bed and, as a reward for shaving myself, he

105

allowed me one of his Salvation Specials, which have been known to twitch a man back from the very brink of the grave. No Jeevesian Worcester sauce and raw eggs for Jock: his potion is simply a dexedrin dissolved in gin and tonic to which he adds a spoonful of Mr Andrew's noted Liver Salts, two effervescing Vitamin C tablets and two ditto Alka-Seltzer. I have little time for foreigners but I must say that Drs Alka and Seltzer should have won the Nobel Prize years ago; my only quarrel with their brain-child is its *noise*.

I was just in time for luncheon, where Eric's shining morning face was much to the fore and Johanna . . . well, smiled at me politely. In the ordinary way I can do great damage to a plate of Jersey *Pais de Mai*, which is a sort of bubble-and-squeak made of potatoes, French beans and onions, fried into a cake and served with little pork sausages, but today the gastric juices simply would not flow and I could only wincingly watch the others eating great store of it while I worked out problems in topology with a hot roll.

Eric took me aside afterwards.

'If you should be feeling a little *effete*,' he said carefully, 'after our sing-song last night . . .?'

'You have a gift for words, Eric. I have never felt effeter. Say on.'

'I have heard it said that a little Pastis is sovereign in these cases. Drives away the evil humours.'

My better judgement rebelled but, as ever, my better judgement received what Jock calls a 'root up the sump' and soon the Pastis was smoothing out the wrinkles in my spleen in cavalry style. When the door-bell rang, two drinks later, I hardly jumped at all. George and Sam entered, snuffing the air curiously.

'Takin' up chemistry?' asked George.

'I have been gargling,' I said stiffly. 'I have a sore throat.'

'To name but a few, I'd say,' said Sam.

'Shall we go?' I said. 'Eric, you'll be able to amuse yourself, won't you? Jock will show you where everything is. Ask for a map if you want to go for a stroll; a man can get lost for months in these Jersey lanes.'

We drove towards St Helier. Where we were going was to the Headquarters of the Paid Police, situated in a street called, bafflingly, *Rouge Bouillon*. Our purpose was to do a delicate deal with a senior officer recommended for his discretion by our sturdy Centenier.

My conscience had been clear for nearly eighteen months, but still I felt a certain unease at entering this Cop-shop; an unease, I must say, soon dispelled by the friendly courtesy extended to us on every hand, with scarcely a chink from a hip-pocketed handcuff. Courteously refusing many an offer of cups of tea, we found ourselves presently in the office of the senior officer in question. I knew him at once for an honest man: my trained eye priced his suit at £40 and dated it as five years old. Bent policemen the world over may hide their guilty gains in the very vaults of Zurich itself, but they cannot resist the mohair suitings, the hand-made shoes. *Experto crede*.

His nostrils twitched delicately.

'My friend has been gargling,' said Sam. 'He has a sore throat.'

'Bad luck,' he said to George.

'Not me; him,' said George, pointing rudely.

'Oh. Well. Now, what can I do to help? It's about these rapes, I understand.'

With a glance at the others, I took it upon myself to be spokesman. He quite liked our reasoning about the rapist's motivation and selectiveness and made a few notes. He explained how his activities were curtailed by the protocol between the Paid and Honorary police – whom he seemed rather to approve of.

'Obviously,' he said, 'there's a bit of friction and frustration; it's natural between professionals and amateurs, but we could never police the country areas in the way that they do – they've got what amounts to a complete Secret Service out there in the *cotils* – and their, ah, summary way of sorting out minor felonies saves us an enormous amount of time and trouble. Every time one of my officers has to testify in court I have to change the whole bloody duty-roster, do you realize that? But I can't interfere in Parish affairs without being asked, any more than Scotland Yard can send men down to a country murder until the local flatfoots admit they're baffled. Having trodden all over the evidence first,' he added bitterly.

Then I told him about our proposed vigilante scheme, carefully omitting to mention our first, abortive try. His brow darkened a bit but he admitted that, there again, it wasn't his business.

'Unless, of course,' he said distinctly, 'anyone was foolish enough to carry weapons on such an expedition.'

We raised hands in horror at the very thought.

Then I broached the real subject of our visit: what we were going to do that night – and what we wanted him to do about it. He laughed at first, then he scowled, then he went a bit purple and raised his voice. I cannot truthfully say that he raved, but he certainly threw himself about a goodish bit. I just went on remorselessly reiterating the logic of the plan, the trifling harm it could do, the possible prophylactic effect, the willingness of the Honorary Police to cooperate if he would join in, the credit which would redound to his Force. He began to see reason; he was not really an unimaginative man. He stuck at one thing, however; he had to have a better indemnity for himself. It was, after all, his career, you understand.

That was when George surprised me – not for the first time.

'Use your phone?' he asked. 'Thanks. Hullo? No, not his secretary, thanks. No, nor his aide-de-camp. Just say it's George Breakspear and that it's urgent. What? Ah, hello, Porky, sorry to wake you up, ha ha; look, you remember that nonsense I told you we were thinking of trying on? Well, Mortdecai's got a man over who understands all about such rubbish and we're all set but the Commander of Detectives here quite naturally feels he needs a bit of higher clearance. Would you have a word with him?'

He had a word with him. The Commander did not actually stand to attention but one felt that, had he been alone, he might have done so. His end of the conversation consisted of seventeen 'yessirs', eight 'of course, sirs' and three 'thank you, sirs'. Then he hung up the telephone and looked at us sternly.

'Well,' he said, 'your friend seems to agree with me that perhaps something might be arranged on the lines you suggest.' We kept our faces solemn. Then we got down to battle-orders, liaised with Connétables and people on the telephone, arranged time-schedules.

'Above all,' I said as we were leaving, 'see that your men do not attempt to arrest the large, ugly man called Jock. First, he would hurt them badly and second, he is not in on the deal.'

'Did I agree to that?'

'Surely it was understood. He's only my servant, you see.'

'Has he any record on the Island?'

'None whatever, I promise you. Just hates having his fingerprints taken.'

'Hmph. All right.'

As we were leaving the main entrance a uniformed sergeant neatly cut me out of the mob and asked whether I could give the Commander a few minutes more of my time – alone. Quaking with guilt and terror I told the others that I would take a taxi home, then I followed the broad-based sergeant back to the C of D's office.

'It's all right, Mr Mortdecai,' he said, 'sit down. You needn't worry. I won't pretend I don't know who you are but I have no quarrel with you. That I know of.' He let that sink in a little.

'What I wanted was to ask you a couple of questions that I couldn't very well ask your friends, since their wives were victims, you understand.'

I didn't understand.

'Well, I'm not too happy about saying positively that all these offences are by the same artist. There's been another one, by the way, here in St Helier, but we've kept it out of the papers and the victim passed out: no description at all. But you know, these things catch on, they sort of become a fashion. It's like little boys setting old ladies on fire in dark alleys – one of them does it and they all think they've got to.'

I shuddered. Some of my best friends have been old ladies – not to mention little boys.

'Now,' he went on, 'we got a semen smear from the doctor's wife and your Centenier contrived to get one from Mrs Davenant's sheets – oh aye, your Centenier isn't half as thick as he likes to pretend – and they're both from the same class of secretor. But that's like saying that they're both blood-group "O". And, as you know, Mr Breakspear was adamant about that sort of thing with regard to Mrs Breakspear, and we couldn't get one from the new victim for reasons I needn't go into. So we haven't even got a third vector.'

I knew what he was going to ask, of course, but I wasn't going to help him, was I?

'I don't understand how I can help you,' I said.

'Well, put it like this. Your lady-wife knows both of the ladies violated in your neighbourhood, right? Well, do you think they might have mentioned anything to her about the assailant's er, personal details, which they might not have cared to tell their husbands?'

'I quite fail to follow you,' I lied.

'Oh yes you bloody do,' he snarled. 'I mean size of male member, whether circumcized, any little peculiarities; things like that.'

'Oh, I see. Oh dear. Use your phone? Hullo, Johanna? Look . . .'

'All right,' she said after a while, 'but "yech".'

'We don't say "yech" in the United Kingdom,' I said, 'we say "faugh".'

'We only say that on the golf-course, but O.K. And I'll try to do the other thing. It may take some time; I'll have to have a Cosy Chat with the cow Sonia.'

'Girl talk,' I said whimsically.

'Faugh!' she said, pronouncing it perfectly.

'This may take a few minutes,' I said to the Commander, looking at him meaningfully. He knew what I meant, he hoisted a great 40-oz bottle of some nameless Scotch on to his desk and raised his eyebrows. I inclined a gracious head. He found two tooth-glasses; they looked a little insanitary but Scotch whisky kills all known germs, as every housewife knows.

Johanna rang back about eight fluid ounces later and rattled off her news in a distant and faintly amused voice.

'That all?' I asked.

'What do you want – blue movies?'

'Good-bye,' I said.

'Good-bye,' she said, 'and Charlie, remember to brush your teeth tonight, huh?'

I hung up and collected my thoughts.

'My wife has recollected things that Mrs Davenant said to her shortly after the assault,' I told the Commander. 'She has also spoken to Mrs Breakspear and to the doctor's wife. The evidence appears, on the face of it, to be conflicting. Violet Davenant said "he was huge, like a horse, he hurt me terribly". Sonia Breakspear describes her assailant as "nothing to write to mother about" and the doctor's wife says, "I don't know – do you mean they come in different sizes?" She's lying, of course; she was a nurse, you see, and all nurses who marry doctors instantly become virgins *ex officio*, it's an understood thing.'

'I have heard that,' he said.

'But Johanna thinks that if he had been something out of the ordinary in any way she would have said something.'

'Yes.'

'As to circumcision, Violet wouldn't have known what one was talking about, Sonia says it wasn't relevant, whatever that means, and the doctor's wife says she thinks "yes". Doesn't help us much, does it?'

'No, not really. Tells us more about the ladies than the rapist, if you follow me, sir.'

We gazed at each other.

'Just so,' is what I said in the end. When I left, shortly afterwards, he behaved as though he felt he had made a friend. For my part, I had reservations.

I didn't have to take a taxi home after all, they lent me a police-car complete with driver. On arrival I offered him a pound note, which he sturdily refused. He wouldn't take a drink, either; he must have thought that I was a spy from the Promotions Board, bless him. What he would accept, to give to the Police Sports Fund, was a bottle of Cyprus sherry which one of us had inadvertently won in a 'raffle' if you know what that is. I felt a pang for whichever athlete won the noxious pottle, but after all, they know the risks when they join the Force, don't they?

How you deal with the tongue of an ox is as follows: you bid the butcher keep it in his pickle-tub for a fortnight, brushing aside his tearful pleas that it should be taken out after eight days. Then you rinse it lovingly and thrust it into the very smallest casserole that will contain it, packing the interstices with many an onion, carrot and other pot-herb. Cover it with heel-taps of wine, beer, cider and, if your cook will let you, the ripe, rich jelly from the bottom of the dripping-pot. Let it ruminate in the back of your oven until you can bear it no longer; whip it out, transfix it to a chopping-board with a brace of forks and – offer up grateful prayers to Whomever gave tongues to the speechless ox. (You can, of course, let it grow cold, when it will slice more delicately, but you will find that you can eat less of it.)

What I am trying to suggest, in my clumsy way, is that we had hot tongue for dinner, along with deliciously bitter turnip-tops and a *Pomme Duchesse* or two for the look of the thing. Eric and Johanna acquitted themselves nobly but I fancy I was well up amongst the leaders.

111

Later, sinking back amongst the cushions and the apricot brandy, I detected a jarring note. Jock, clearing away the broken meats, was now wearing a black Jersey or Guernsey, a pair of black slacks, black running-shoes and all the signs of a man who might well be carrying a deadly weapon.

'What's this?' I cried. 'What's this? Have you been watching the television again? I've told you and *told* you . . . '

'We're going out tonight, Mr Charlie, aren't we? Going to *chapel*, remember?'

In truth I had quite forgotten. I shall not pretend that the ox-tongue turned to ashes in my belly but it certainly started to give signs of discontent with its lot.

'We'll have to put it off, Jock; I forgot to get the cockerel.'

'Me and Farver Eric collected it 's'afternoon. Lovely bird it is, too, black as your hat.'

I drank all the coffee that was left and bolted the pill which Jock slipped me. Then, as is my wont when attending Satanic Masses in draughty medieval chapels, I packed a few iron rations such as liqueur Scotch, a paper of pheasant sandwiches and a small jar of *Pâté de Lièvre* into a briefcase; adding, after reflection, a pair of coarse warm pyjamas – who knew where I might spend the night? – and, mindful of Johanna's admonition, a toothbrush and tooth-powder.

We drove to George's house and collected Sam and him, both of them grumbling and sulking, then off we all sped on a total of eight wheels: Jock and Eric in my Mini, which was to be their get-away vehicle, and the rest of us in George's large, capable, boring Rover. Just before we left I was kind enough to ask George whether his Rover was licensed, taxed, oiled and possessed of a Roadworthiness Certificate. He looked at me pityingly, of course, but I'm used to that. People are always looking at me pityingly; it's because they think I'm potty, you see. Off, as I say, we sped through the night towards La Hougue Bie and were soon elaborately lost, which is a surprisingly easy thing to do in Jersey because all the country roads, thanks to something called *La Visite du Branquage*, look exactly the same. Indeed, getting lost in Jersey is one of the few outdoor sports one can enjoy in the colder evenings: it's tough on petrol but it saves you a fortune in other ways. None of us got very cross except, of course, George. When we finally pitched up at the site we parked the Rover at a discreet distance; Jock, it seemed, had already secreted the Mini in some furtive backwater which he had previously reconnoitred. We foregathered at the main gate. It really wasn't worth diddling the padlock: George did a splendid Army-style gate-vault and I, full of stinking pride, followed suit and bruised my belly badly. Sam and Eric, long purged of any competitive spirit, simply crept between the bars. I didn't see what Jock did, he's a professional – he simply materialized beside us in the dark.

We huddled together glumly, just inside the gate, while Jock loped off soundlessly into the night, feather-footed as any questing vole, to ascertain that the honest proprietaries of the ossuaries were abed. It seemed a very long time before he reappeared.

'Sorry, Mr Charlie, but there was this courting couple, see, and I had to put the fear into them, didn't I? See them off, see?'

'And are they quite gone now?'

He looked at me miffedly. When Jock sees people off, they stay seen off.

'Yes, Mr Charlie. Off like bleeding rabbits, him still holding his trousers up, her leaving certain garments behind in a wasteful fashion which I happen to have in my pocket this moment if you wish to check.'

I shuddered delicately, told him I would take his word for it.

Urged by a now surly George and Sam, we made our way over to the great mound itself, that horrid pile of the guts of ages long-gone and never to be one-half comprehended. Jock busied himself briefly with the padlock and chain which guarded the entrance to the underground passage leading to the grave-chamber and disappeared with Eric, my tape-recorder and a plastic bag full of the best toads available. When they emerged we all made our way up the winding path which leads to the chapels crowning the mound. Jock was as good as his word: the lock of the Jerusalem Chapel fell to his bow and spear with no more protest than a subdued clunk.

Eric bustled into the chapel in a business-like way, as one to the manner born. George, Sam and I followed him with different degrees of reticence. The rooster had been fed with raisins soaked in rum by Jock: I wish to make it clear that it was not I who carried it. Eric wasted no time; he dabbed little bits of this and that on the remains of the ancient altar and then spread over it his splendid corporal. The rest of us huddled, a little sheepishly perhaps, at the back of the tiny chancel – no larger than a bathroom in the better kind of country house. When I say 'the rest of us' I exclude Jock, of course, who was lurking somewhere in the shadows of the porch – his favourite place in times of turpitude and quite right too.

Strong though we were of purpose, I suspect that a show of hands, had it been taken at that moment, would have indicated a pretty *nem. con.* desire to return home and forget the whole thing. Except for Eric. He was growing almost visibly, taking on the stature of the craftsman who knows that what he is doing is not a thing that anyone else could do better; the dignity, if you like, of a scientist devising a hydrogen bomb, torn by the knowledge of evil but driven by the compulsion of research and the jackboot of human history.

'You will now be silent!' he suddenly said in a voice of such authority that we all stood up straight. He was wearing a long, white *soutane* sort of thing made of heavy silk; the only illumination came from the single candle he had placed on the altar: an ordinary white one, I noticed, and the right way up. Any mumbo-jumbo, it was evident, was not likely to embody the word 'abracadabra'. The candle lit up only the text of the travesty of the Mass before him and a small but startling patch of the embroidery on the corporal.

He said, or seemed to say, a few sentences under his breath. I did not try to hear, I have troubles of my own. Then, in a high, clear voice, he began to patter out the Introit, with the canting, carneying kind of intonation that old-fashioned Irish priests used to use – and still do for all I know. I dare say Sam may have picked up some of the Latin nastinesses that started to creep into the Ritual but I'm sure they were all Greek to George. I, who had both copied and, later, typed out, the Ritual, was expecting these passages, but nevertheless, on Eric's lips they seemed to sound nastier every minute. When he came to the part which, in Lord Dunromin's MS, had been filled only with a rectangle of red ink containing the words *Secrets Infâmes*, his voice, startlingly, dropped quite two octaves and in a horrid, bass grunt he began rhythmically to intone a number of names beginning with Ashtaroth, Astarte, Baal, Chemoz – people like that. I am happy to say that I do not remember more than a few of them – and if I did I certainly should not write them down here: I am not a superstitious man but I do not believe in poking sleeping gods in the eye with a sharp stick. I'm sure you understand me.

We three others had all, I suppose, been prepared for a mixture of tedium and embarrassment but it was quite extraordinary how little Eric Tichborne exuded a sort of aura of command – extraordinary, too, how he changed in stature. When his voice returned to the canting, seminary-priest's whine the inflections seemed to rise and fall in an almost inhuman way which I seemed to have heard before. On the previous night. Coming from my own tape-recorder. I did not like it a bit.

During the particularly tasteless mockery of the *Kyrie Eleison* his voice seemed to be shaking with an emotion which could have been suppressed laughter or, indeed, suppressed tears. Certainly not Pastis. But the strangest thing came afterwards, for his speech seemed to accelerate to a point where he was rattling off words at a speed which one would not have thought the human voice-box capable of. It went on accelerating until it had become the unnerving twitter of – yes – of a tape-recorder played at too fast a speed. This suddenly, inexplicably, broke off and we could hear the agonized rasp of his breathing. This, too, changed, as we watched and listened, and as he bowed and cramped into a spasm apparently asthmatic: wrenching coughs and retchings racked his little frame and, in between, he yelled out bits of Ezekiel: ' . . . *young men riding upon horses . . . there were her breasts pressed . . . there she bruised the teats of her virginity . . .* '

George half-rose and looked at me with a question. I shook my head. This was not something to interfere with. Bit by bit the little broken priest re-assembled himself, leaned upon the altar and pursued the increasingly filthy Ritual but more and more as though the words hurt him physically. It was probably an illusion caused by the candle-flame, but it seemed to me that he was being buffeted about by something that could not have been a wind. I stole a glance at the others: George's face was a mask of disapproval and disgust, his mouth not quite closed. Sam, to my astonishment, displayed a face crumpled up with compassion and, if I was not mistaken, traced with tears.

I don't know what my own face looked like.

Up at the altar, only his hands clearly visible in the pool of candlelight, Fr Tichborne jerked and swayed as his voice grew ever shriller, more frantic. I did not ask the others, afterwards, what they saw but to my mind the light seemed to thicken. I became acutely conscious, all of a sudden, of being exactly above the grave-chamber of the dolmen. Through the soles of my feet I seemed to feel a grinding crepitation as though the great slabs of the roof underground were shifting against the slabs of the side-walls. I am very much grown up, mature and not in the least superstitious, but I don't mind admitting that I wished, just then, that I were young enough to wish that my mother were there, if you take my meaning. Not that she would have helped, of course; she wasn't that kind of mother.

Something was being burned on the altar now, something which gave off a thick, delicious smoke that muddled our thoughts. The rooster was produced and displayed and then certain beastly things happened to it which, in an ordinary time and place, I dare say we should have prevented. The priest turned round to us, arms raised, his gown now kilted up above his navel to keep it clear of the blood-stains. George turned completely around, his face sunk in his hands. Sam did not move but I could hear him whimpering very quietly, piteously. I am, as I have often pointed out, a mature and sensible man; moreover I had personally copied out the Ritual and knew what was coming – I was a little surprised, therefore, to find that I had crossed the fingers of both my hands.

It cannot have been Eric's voice which began to bellow Great Salute and Imprecation of *S. Sécaire*: so little a man could never have whooped and bayed in so disgusting a fashion, nor can I believe that the rocks beneath the chapel could have shifted and groaned so hideously as they seemed to. In that thick, stupefying atmosphere, amidst those atavistic animal noises, nothing was real and when Eric seemed to rise some eight inches from the floor my fuddled surprise was only that I had not seen that he was barefooted and had not known that his right foot was horribly deformed. He was stuttering out the list of things which *S. Sécaire* offers to those against whom he is invoked when I saw his face blacken. He fell towards us on his face. His face, when it struck the stone floor, made a sound which I have been trying to forget ever since. It was inches from my shoe. The silk robe was almost up to his armpits; his body was not good to look at. He went on making odd noises – how was I to know that he was dead?

In any case, it was just then that the door burst open and all sorts of Centeniers, Vingteniers, Connétable's officers, aye and

116

even members of the dread Paid Police themselves, thronged in and arrested every one of us again and again.

Now, according to my plans, you see, we should have been neatly arrested, charged with breaking and entering, and fined some five bob each the next day, giving enough details to enable the *Jersey Evening Post* to make it known to one and all – and particularly, of course, to the witchmaster rapist chap – that the Mass of St Sécaire had in fact been held, with him as the objective. I had, perhaps rather coyly, not made it perfectly clear to George and Sam that we should probably all have to spend the night in durance vile: that is to say, what you and I call 'the nick' – I don't like to cause people premonitory pain, do you? – and of course they would not, in any case, have agreed to the notion.

As it turned out, neither Sam nor George had really pulled himself together before we arrived at the Cop-shop in Rouge Bouillon, nor did they fully understand that they were to be the involuntary guests of the Deputy Lieutenant and Commander-in-Chief of Jersey until they – we – were issued with two blankets apiece, a cup of cocoa and a capital piece of bread and dripping, which I for one was ready for. Luckily, there were plenty of cells – the tourist season had scarcely begun – so that I had one all to myself and was spared any recriminations which my friends might otherwise, in the heat of the moment, have thought fit to heap upon me. The infinitely kindly policeman-gaoler permitted me to keep my briefcase of pyjamas, sandwiches and Scotch, exacting only a token tribute from the last. I shall not pretend that I slept well but at least I brushed my teeth, unlike some I could name.

12

Where the dead red leaves of the years lie rotten,
The cold old crimes and the deeds thrown by,
The misconceived and the misbegotten,
I would find a sin to do ere I die,
Sure to dissolve and destroy me all through . . .

The Triumph of Time

We who assembled in the Commander's office at half-past eight the next morning were but a moody crew. George and Sam seemed to be harbouring some petty resentment about the fact that I had had the simple foresight to pack my toothbrush and things. Perhaps, too, they just didn't like being locked up: there are people like that.

George was stalking up and down, four paces to the left, four to the right, like the captain of a very small ship pacing whatever it is that master-mariners pace. He was snarling a string of names of influential people, all of whom, he made it clear, he was about to telephone, and in the order named. Sam sat in a sort of collapsed lump: like me, he is a lovely talker when he has had his pre-luncheon drinks, but not before, really.

When George had exhausted his mental address-book, the Commander of Detectives cleared his throat in a way that gave the merest hint of smugness.

'Grave charges,' he said. 'Graver, perhaps, than you realize. Certainly graver than we had anticipated. Serious view they'll take of it. Serious. Unacceptable, you see.'

Sam made a brief reference to the Southern end of the digestive tract, in the plural, then relapsed into his lump.

'No, no, sir,' said the C of D, 'that doesn't help a bit, not that attitude doesn't. Constructive is the word. Let's be constructive. See what we can work out. Least harmful, least publicity, least cost to the taxpayer, eh?'

Sam made a suggestion which might or might not have given pleasure to the average taxpayer.

'There you are again, you see, sir. Interesting biologically but not what you'd call constructive. Lucky we haven't got a police stenographer in here, eh?' The gentle threat floated gently to the ground. Sam grumbled, 'Sorry', and George said, 'Hrrmph'. I said that I wasn't used to drinking cocoa for breakfast. The C of D produced his whisky bottle in an insulting fashion.

Then he explained to us, with thinly-disguised relish, that we were up an improbably-named creek in a concrete canoe without a paddle and that the kindest thing he could do, before clapping us into his deepest dungeon, was to allow us to make one telephone call each. George's advocate, the grandest imaginable, kept on saying 'oh dear, oh dear', until George slammed the instrument down. Sam's advocate seemed to be saying 'oy oy, oy oy' until Sam told him curtly that he wanted no moaning at the bar.

My own chap is but a mere solicitor and his reaction was crisp. 'Put the copper on,' he said, crisply.

Two minutes later the C of D told us, crisply, that it had just occurred to him that he couldn't hold us until he could think of some better charges and that, if we were prepared to go through a trifling formality at the box-office, we were free to go for the time being.

We went. I was prepared to chat freely on the way home but the others seemed both tacit and mute. I shall never understand people.

At home, Johanna greeted me with her cryptic smile, the one that makes her look like a rich man's Mona Lisa, and the sisterly sort of kiss with which a wife tells you that she loves you; but. Scorning explanations, I swept off to my dressing-room, leaving instructions that I should be called at twenty minutes before luncheon.

'Yes, dear,' she said. She has a gift for words.

In the event it was Jock who aroused me from a hoggish slumber, which had been intermingled with fearful dreams.

'Chops, Mr Charlie,' he said, 'and chips and them little French beans.'

'You interest me strangely. By the way, Jock, did you make good your escape last night without any, ah, friction?'

'Escape?' he sneered. 'That lot couldn't catch VD in Port Said.'

'*Please*, Jock. I wish to enjoy my luncheon.'

'Yeah. Well, cook's just turned the chops over so you got about four minutes to get downstairs, I reckon.'

I made it. I remember the chops vividly, they were delicious; so were them little French beans.

The afternoon hummed with telephone calls; I felt like W. B. Yeats in his bee-loud glade. First George, who upbraided me sternly, saying that Sonia had been quite frantic at being left alone all night. ('Pooh' is what I mentally said to that.) He was full of plans to import the flower of the English Bar to cow the Royal Court of Jersey.

'Don't be so damn silly,' I said; 'for one thing, they'd probably have no standing here; for another it would take them years to learn the quirks and quiddities of Jersey law. Leave it alone. Trust your Uncle Charlie.'

'Now, look here, Mortdecai,' he began. I explained courteously that I never listened to sentences beginning with those words. He started again, and again I had to interrupt him to explain that, although no great churchgoer, I found blasphemy distasteful. He breathed heavily into the instrument for perhaps half a minute. I felt that I should help him.

'The weather, I believe, is fine for the time of the year, is it not?'

He hung up. I started the *Times* crossword.

Sam was the next to telephone.

'Charlie, are you quite insane or do you really know what you're about? George says you're talking like a lunatic.'

'Have I ever let you down?' I asked simply.

'Have I ever given you the chance before?'

'How is Violet?'

'In complete withdrawal. Diagnosis: not sure. Prognosis: can't say. Being fed intravenously. Change the subject.'

'All right. We had chops for luncheon. Come to dinner: Jock is making Aloo Ghosht Bangalore with his own hands.'

'Charlie, I suppose you realize that if you haven't got this thing right I may have to disembowel you with my own hands?'

'Of course. But if I haven't got it right you may not need to, you see. Come to dinner?'

'Oh, all right. Eight o'clock?'

'Come earlier. Let's get sloshed.'

'All right.'

Johanna, who had wandered in, said, 'How nice to have one's friends in so often.'

'Tell Jock to put some more potatoes in the curry,' I said. 'Dear.'

The next call was the one I was dreading: it was from Jolly Solly my Wonder Solicitor.

'Ho ho ho!' he cried happily, rubbing his hands. (He has one of those loudspeaker telephones which leave both hands free – indispensable for confirmed hand-rubbers.) 'Ho ho! Such an interesting mess as you're in I never hoped to live to see. Legal history we shall make!'

'Less chortling and more news,' I demanded sourly.

'Ah, yes, well, you're naturally anxious. By the way, you've no aged parents whose grey hairs you might bring down in sorrow to the grave? No? Well, that's good news, I suppose. The rest is mostly bad. They're not yet sure how many charges they'll bring against you, half the clerks in the Attorney-General's office are working day and night on it, smacking their lips over the dripping roast. The preliminary list of choices is as follows:

'Breaking and Entering.

'Acting in a manner likely to cause a breach of the peace.

'Foul and disgusting language.

'Obstructing a Police Officer in the execution of his duty.

'Sacrilege under Section 24 of the Larceny Act of 1914: that carries a maximum sentence of life imprisonment, bet you didn't know that, ha ha.

'Sedition, well, yes, arguable.

'*Art. I de la Loi pour Empêcher le Mauvais Traitement des Animaux* – that only carries three months. Oh yes, and a £200 fine.

'*Art. I de la Loi Modifiant le Droit Criminel (Sodomie & Bestialité) confirmée par Ordre de Sa Majesté en Conseil*, I really do hope they don't fix you up for that one: the maximum is life but the *minimum* is three years. Last chap was only deported, but he was potty.

'Theft of one rooster or cockerel – no, the farmer swears Jock didn't pay him for it. You might get that reduced to "Taking and Driving Away without Owner's Permission", ha ha.

'Vagrancy. You didn't have any cash on you, you see.

'Failure to sign a driving licence.

'Breach of the Drugs (Prevention of Misuse) (Jersey) Law of 1964 – that depends on what the stuff Fr Tichborne was burning turns out to be.

'Breach – possibly – of *La Loi sur L'Exercise de la Médecine et Chirurgerie Vétérinaire.*'

I had no time to seek out a looking-glass, nor did I need to: I can say without hesitation that my face was white as any sheet – probably whiter than most.

'That all?' I quavered manfully.

'By no means, Charlie, by no means. I'm afraid that all those can be doubled and redoubled in spades by repeating them with the words "conspiring to" in front of them. Then a number of civil actions would probably lie:

'Trespass to the chapel and damage thereto.

'Trespass to the dolmen and damage thereto.

'Trespass to the Hougue Bie site generally and failure to pay the admission charge.

'Damages in respect of the rooster or cockerel.

'They'll probably think of some more, they've hardly started. Then I'm afraid there's all sorts of sticky possibilities under Ecclesiastical Law – and if that lot brings charges I'd plead guilty outright if I were you: cases in their courts drag out for years and the costs would break you.

'Just for example, if the Bishopric of Coutances hears about it you could be in bad trouble; the Bishop has something called a Right of Interference in anything concerning a priest criminally.

'Then there's a particularly horrid Papal Bull of 1483 which is still in force wherein Pope Sixtus IV protects Jersey churches against all sorts of things with an automatic sentence of "excommunication, anathema, eternal malediction and confiscation of property". Shouldn't worry too much about that unless you happen to be a

Papist – the confiscation of property bit wouldn't hold much water today.'

'Oh good,' I said heavily. 'And *now* have you exhausted all the possibilities? I mean, I've heard about the man in New Orleans who's serving 999 years, but I am no longer a young man, you know.'

'Well, as a matter of fact, I'm afraid there could be quite a lot more. You see, there's practically no codified statutory criminal law in Jersey; virtually all offences are Common Law ones. What that means, to the ordinary customer, is that the Attorney–General can prosecute you for anything deemed offensive or anti-social simply by sticking the word "unlawfully" in front of a description of whatever it was that you did and was objected to. Do you follow me?'

I whimpered assent.

'But let me bring a little sunshine into your life. All domestic motor insurance policies are automatically invalidated when the vehicle is used for an illegal purpose, so they'll certainly nab George Breakspear for driving uninsured. Yes, I thought that might cheer you up a bit. Oh, and by the way, you're lucky that your nasty little ceremony didn't actually succeed in raising up the Devil in person: there's a foot-and-mouth restriction in force at the moment and they would have got you under the Diseases of Animals Act for transporting a cloven-footed beast without a licence, ha ha.'

'Yes, ha ha indeed. In the meantime, what do I do?'

'Wait,' he said, 'and pray.'

I hung up.

Neither waiting nor praying is a skill I can boast of. Thinking was what was required – but thinking requires Scotch whisky, as all great thinkers agree and I had, in an idle moment, made an absurd promise to Johanna. The clock stood at ten to three. I turned the hands on to five-past six and rang the bell for Jock. He brought in the life-giving drinks-tray in what I can only call an insubordinate manner and wordlessly corrected the clock.

'Jock,' I said as the decanter gurgled, 'I rather fancy I am in the shit. It's because of Fr Tichborne dying, you see. Difficult to control the thing now.'

'Wasn't his fault, was it?' said Jock sulkily.

'Of course not, he was an excellent chap, the soul of courtesy; wouldn't have dreamed of embarrassing us on purpose. But the fact remains that it's made everything very difficult. What's to be done?'

'Well, kissing goes by favour, dunnit? Specially in Jersey.'

'I've never really known what that means. What do you take it to mean?'

'Well, say, if the filth' (by which he meant the CID), 'is getting a bit too close to you, you ring up one of your mates who was at Borstal with you and he fits the copper up with a corruption rap. Doesn't matter if it don't stick: they have to suspend him till it's investigated and the new bloke they put on your case hasn't got his contacks, has he, and most of what the first bloke had he kept in his head, didn't he, so you got a couple of munce to sort things out, see?'

'I think I see. Goodness. But I suppose it's the way of the world. I certainly can't think of anything else. Thank you, Jock.'

I rang up George.

'George,' I said in dulcet tones, 'I really must apologize for my incivility just now. Heat of the moment, you understand. Not myself, eh?'

I accepted his grunt as an acceptance of my apology.

'It seems to me,' I went on, 'that our watchword must be "kissing goes by favour" – we must use our *influence*, bring gentle pressure to bear, don't you think? For instance, how well do you know the more august chaps in Jersey; were you at Borst . . . I mean Harrow with any of them? I mean chaps like the chap you rang up from the Police Station yesterday?'

'Very well indeed, some of them.'

'Well, there you are then. Ask them to tea, fill them up with *tuck* – hot buttered crumpets, little meat pies, cherry brandy – all the nice things they won't be allowed to have at home – then remind them of your schooldays together, all those innocent pranks, you know the sort of thing.'

'I am doing precisely that at this moment. Is there anything else?'

'No, not really.'

'Good-bye, then.'

'Good-bye, George.'

The thought of hot buttered crumpets took me by the throat like a tigress: I was racked with desire for them. I strolled into the kitchen, where I found Jock sticking photographs of Shirley Temple into his scrap-book.

'Jock,' I said casually, 'do you suppose there are any hot buttered crumpets in the house?' He glowered at me.

'You know perfickly well what Mrs Mortdecai said about hot buttered crumpets, Mr Charlie. "Better without them" is what she said you was.'

'But this is a special case,' I whined. 'I *need* those crumpets, can't you see that?'

His face remained stony.

'Tell you what, Jock; you forget to mention hot buttered crumpets to Mrs Mortdecai and I'll forget to mention about you pinching her caviare. Kissing goes by favour, you know.' He sighed.

'You catch on quick, Mr Charlie.'

I drew up a chair, rubbing my hands like any lawyer.

For some arcane reason the crumpets they sell in Jersey tend to come in packets of seven, which means that when two crumpet-eaters are gathered together there is a rather sordid gobbling-race for he who finishes his third crumpet before his contender has a natural right to the fourth. We were both well into our third – it looked like being a photo-finish – when the door-bell rang and Jock arose, glumly wiping the melted butter off his chin. It is at times like these that breeding shows. After a rapid mental battle I divided the remaining crumpet into two almost equal halves.

Jock returned, flashed a glance at the muffineer, and announced that some gentlemen from the Press were in the lobby and should he show them into the drawing-room.

The gentlemen of the Press proved to be one personable young woman from the *Jersey Evening Post*, clearly bursting with intelligence, one world-weary young photographer and one large, sad, well-bred chap representing wireless and television. I dealt out glasses of ardent spirits with the deftness of a Mississippi steamboat gambler, then made a deal with them.

'Keep the national press off our backs,' was the burden of my song, 'and you shall have, exclusively, all the information and photographs you can reasonably expect. Fail me in this and

I shall close my doors upon you and Tell All to the *Sunday People*.'

Three shudders followed this, then three fervent nods.

In carefully rehearsed words I told them quite a lot of the truth, bearing down heavily on the fact that the offender was clearly a witchmaster and that it was well known that the *Messe de S. Sécaire* could not fail to draw his teeth and rob him of his mystic powers if he were a true witch and that, if he persisted in his evil-doing, certain of his physical powers would also be grievously afflicted.

Then I darted over to the other half of the house and borrowed from my landlord a large, smelly pipe and a small, smelly poodle. With the one clenched between my teeth (yes, the pipe) and the other snuggled in my arms, I allowed them to take photographs of benign old Mortdecai in his favourite armchair and benigner old Mortdecai pottering about in the garden. They went away quite satisfied. I fled to the bathroom and got rid of the taste of the pipe with mouthwash, changed my clothes and told Jock to send the poodle-polluted suit to the cleaners or, if beyond redemption, to the poor.

Nothing else of any note happened that day except the exquisite curry, thoughout which I played records of Wagner: he goes beautifully with curry, the only use I've ever found for him. Sam left early and I too was ready for my bed, as I always am after a night in the cells. I heard Johanna come in from her bridge-party but she went straight to her room, so I suppose she had lost. I lay awake for a long time, thinking of poor little Eric Tichborne and feeling like a pagan suckled in a creed outworn. I dare say you know the feeling, especially if your wife sometimes goes to bed without saying good night.

13

Seven sorrows the priests give their Virgin;
But thy sins, which are seventy times seven,
Seven ages would fail thee to purge in,
And then they would haunt thee in heaven:
Fierce midnights and famishing morrows,
And the loves that complete and control
All the joys of the flesh, all the sorrows
That wear out the soul.

Dolores

I spend the morning and much of the afternoon in bed, moping and pretending to be poorly. Jock brought me no less than three successive cups of his delicious beef-tea, not to mention a sandwich or two from time to time. Johanna tried to take my temperature.

'Oh no you don't!' I cried.

'But we always take it like that in the States.'

I was saved by the bell of the telephone: the Attorney-General's staff wanted to know about my citizenship status. Then it rang again: it was George, whose advocate had been terrifying him. I told him that my solicitor was a much better terrifier and a faster – he had done all his terrifying the previous day. Then it rang again and I told the Chief Superintendent's clerk that, no I couldn't pop down to the Station, I was suffering from a tertiary ague.

This sort of thing went on. There will, I think, be telephones in Hell.

127

What I was waiting for was the *Jersey Evening Post*, for a good press was essential to the efficacy of our scheme and might well be useful when things came to be considered in Court.

Our copy of the newspaper is delivered at six o'clock but, evidently, other people get theirs earlier, for the telephone calls started again with redoubled vigour at half-past four. Set out in rough order they comprised:

One learned Rector of my acquaintance who wished, sadly and probably sensibly, that we had tried the Church's resources first, instead of imperilling our souls by flirting with the Opposition.

One Christian Scientist – I thought they had all died out – who explained that rape was all in the mind and merely a manifestation of Mortal Error. She was still talking when I hung up on her, but I don't suppose she noticed.

Three separate and distinct Jehovah's Witnesses who told me that Armageddon was scheduled for 1975 and that there would be no place for me among the 50,000 survivors unless I did something about the state of my soul pretty smartly. I didn't try to explain that the thought of surviving in a world populated only by Witnesses horrified me: I just gave them each a telephone number of one boring friend or another who would, I assured them, relish a visit from one of their sect.

Two respectable acquaintances who each had found that they had invited us to dinner on the wrong day and would ring us back in due course.

Three ditto who had accepted invitations from us but now found they had previous – or more likely subsequent – engagements.

One engaging re-incarnation buff who had been the Great Beast of Revelation the last time around.

One quite frantic chap who said I had got it all wrong about the Devil: 'She's a coloured person,' he explained.

Several alleged and assorted witches, some of whom sneered and some of whom offered alibis.

One drunken Irishman who asked for precise directions to my house so that he could call and bash my bloody brains in.

One chap called Smith who said that he was going to church to pray for my soul but with no very lively expectation of success.

One prominent member of the Pressure Group for the Reform of the Cruelty to Animals Law, who proposed to take the poodle away from me and find it a good home. (I told her that I, too, was keen on cruelty to animals but that the poodle was a stuffed one, alas, having died last year in a nameless fashion.)

Clearly, the *Jersey Evening Post* must have done me proud and, indeed, when my copy at last arrived, so it proved. Bannered and splashed across the front page was all the Mortdecai that was fit to print. The photograph sent Johanna and Jock lurching and staggering across the floor in ribald mirth: senile, scholarly old Mortdecai, be-poodled and be-piped, beamed pottily out at one in the most *diverting* way. Miss H. Glossop, the young lady reportress, had evidently done her homework, for her facts were clear and well-researched. Erudite, unworldly old Mortdecai, it appeared, anxious to help friends in distress, had fought fire with fire to such effect that the very celebrant of the rites had dropped dead – to everyone's regret – at the climax of the performance. 'What,' the story implied, 'would the harvest be for the guilty target, when even the innocent gunner, so to speak, couldn't take the recoil?' Miss Glossop went on in an exceedingly well-informed way to recount the marvellous powers attributed to the Mass of *S. Sécaire*, and to pity the witch who pitted his paltry powers against it. No literate diabolist could possibly have missed the point. Moreover, apart from a slight tendency to freely split infinitives, her style evidently derived from the best models: not a single 'subsequently transpired' marred her pellucid prose. I was well pleased. Indeed, I got up in time for dinner and made a few telephone calls myself. Sam was out – no one knew where – but George grudgingly admitted that the ploy seemed to be going well. Solly, his mouth full (solicitors dine much earlier than barristers), admitted that my image might well be a little better for the publicity, and let me know that one or two of the charges had been dropped and only four or five fresh ones had been thought of.

I began to feel positively chipper. Apart from the prospect of a few score years in prison the horizon was pretty clear. Peals of laughter wafted through from the kitchen, where Jock, I suppose, was showing my photograph to his dominoes-friend and the cook. I beamed indulgently.

Dinner was announced.

I need hardly say that I am not one of those whose minds dwell continually on foodstuffs: but when I do, once in a while, turn my mind in that direction it is with a certain single-mindedness; particularly when, as in this case, the grocery under advisement proves to be a guinea-fowl, that triumph of the poulterer's art. This particular feathered friend was an uncommonly well-poultered example: it must have led a beautiful and sheltered life. Hand-in-hand tripped a bottle of Barolo, singing wistful lays of the gravel slopes of the Piedmont. Seldom have I spent a happier and more innocent hour but, as the Master himself tells us, it is at times like these that Fate creeps out of a dark alley, fingering a stuffed eel-skin destined for the back of one's neck.

I threw the end of my *Romeo y Julieta* into the embers of the fire and cast a sort of husbandly look at Johanna. She raised an eyebrow shaped like a seagull's wing. I winked. The telephone rang.

It was the Centenier. He thought I might like to know that there had been another rape. The wife of the tomato grower. Satanic trapping as before but with an addition: having knocked her unconscious with the same gentle punch, he had scribbled the word 'secretary' in greasepaint in a semi-circle on her bare belly, well below the navel.

'Have you read the paper tonight?' I asked.

'I seen the photo of you, sir, but I 'aven't what you might call perused the entire article, 'aving been called out on this case, eh?'

'Take another look at the lady's tummy,' I said, 'I think you'll find the word is *Sécaire*.'

I rose wearily, feeling as old as sin.

'Ah well,' I sighed, 'back to the grind.'

'Oh *good*,' said Johanna. 'Race you to bed?'

'I did not mean that.'

'You were meaning it just now.'

'Just now I was in early middle age. At this moment I feel ready for the Tom and Geriatric ward.'

'All right, we'll play patients and nurses: you shall chase me upstairs, but very slowly; to husband your strength.'

'Oh, very well,' I said.

My heart was not really in it but I appreciated the fact that she wanted to help. For some reason, you see, we can't talk to each other properly.

14

Not utterly struck spiritless
For shame's sake and unworthiness
Of these poor forceless hands that come
Empty, these lips that should be dumb,
This love whose seal can but impress
These weak word-offerings wearisome
Whose blessings have not strength to bless
Nor lightnings fire to burn up aught
Nor smite with thunders of their thought.

Epilogue

A hideous wailing penetrated my grimly dreams: I awoke shuddering. It was only Jock mounting the stairs with my tea-tray, singing 'On the Good Ship Lollipop' in his best falsetto. He does it rather well but there is a time and place for Shirley Temple.

'This *aubade* or *mattinata* must not occur again, Jock. It hurts me in the liver. "Cursed is he who greets his brother with a loud voice in the morning" as Deuteronomy was so fond of pointing out.'

Vengefully, he allowed some tea to slop into my saucer as he handed it to me, then deliberately mopped it up with a well-ripened pocket-handkerchief. Game, set and match to him. The tea, when I could bring myself to sample it, tasted like waters of Babylon which had been too freely wept in.

'How is the canary this morning?'

'Got a bad leg.'

'Then summon the best vet money can buy, spare no expense. A Mr Blampied is well spoken of.'

'He's bin. Said the leg'll 'ave to come orf.'

'Nonsense. I am not a rich man, I cannot afford to keep wooden-legged canaries in idle luxury.'

'He's a singer, Mr Charlie, not a bleedin' dancer. Oh, yeah, and Mr Davenant and Mr Breakspear are waiting for you downstairs.'

'Oh dear, oh Christ, are they really? Er, they seem in a jolly sort of mood, I dare say?'

'Bloody diabolical.'

'Oh. They'll have heard about the new incident, then?'

'Yeah.'

Jock's gift for language had not failed him: 'diabolical' was the only word to express the moods of George and Sam. They stared at me, as I good-morninged them, as though they were a brace of Lady Macbeths confronted with one of the less acceptable kinds of damned spot. I crinkled my mouth into a wry smile. Their mouths stayed grim. I toyed with the idea of telling them a funny story, then discarded it.

'Drinks?' I asked. 'Scotch? Gin and tonic? Bottled beer?'

'Mortdecai,' said George, 'you are a four-letter man.'

'D'you know, I've never quite known what that meant.'

Sam told me; in four letters. I allow no one to speak to me like that.

'Sam,' I began heavily.

He repeated the word.

'Well,' I conceded, 'there may be something in what you suggest. But consider: the rapist – if this incident *is* his work – may not have had time to read yesterday's *Jersey Evening Post*; it had not been long on the streets.'

'Then how do you account for the word *Sécaire*?'

'Oh. You heard about that bit.'

'Yes, we heard. And it seems to us that your perverse and crack-brained scheme has not only disgraced us and put us in jeopardy of gaol but, worst of all, it has not worked. The man is clearly laughing at us.'

'Early days to be certain of that, surely? I mean, it's just possible that it might *really* work, you know. In his subconscious or something . . .' I tailed off lamely.

'Rubbish. We must simply resume the ambushes – every night from now on. The new incident confirms our view that the targets are always likely to be Englishwomen in their thirties and living in this neighbourhood. It's just a matter of time now, and vigilance.'

'And staff-work,' grunted George.

'And loyalty.'

'I see. Very well. We start tonight, I take it? Or do we leave it a night to let the chap re-charge his, ah, batteries?'

'Tonight,' they said with one voice.

'I suppose you're right; chap like that probably doesn't run off batteries – glands like nuclear reactors, I should think.'

'Unfunny. And I suppose you know that we're all due at the Police Station in forty minutes: I dare say you might care to offer us a drink before we leave.'

I opened my mouth and shut it again. It was clear that I could do no right that morning.

The Chief Superintendent met us with a stony look. Like all good policemen who have received hints to lay off from people in high places, he was in an ugly mood. He studied us carefully, one by one – the time-honoured technique of policemen who wish you to understand that they will be Keeping an Eye on you in the future and that you'd better not be caught parking on a yellow line.

'For some reason not confided in me,' he began heavily, 'it has been decided that this is to be treated as a silly prank which ended tragically. Most of the gravamen of the many charges will be laid to the account of the deceased Tichborne. I hope that will please you. You are only to be charged with Unlawfully Entering Private Premises, Unlawfully Causing Scandal and Distress, Failing to prevent a Breach of the Law Against Ill-treatment of Animals and you, Mr Breakspear, with Driving an Uninsured Vehicle and Failing to Sign a Driving Licence.'

I broke out in a sweat of relief. George grated his teeth audibly. Sam's eyes seemed to be fixed on some distant and loathsome object.

'I have been in touch informally,' the policeman went on, 'with the *Société Jersaise*. They are, quite rightly, shocked and furious, but you may find that a written apology and an offer to pay for a new padlock-chain and for the removal of the smoke-stains on the walls of the chapel will satisfy them. Say, three hundred pounds.'

Three cheque-books flashed in the dusty sunshine; three fountain pens scratched and squirted in unison.

'The Police Court magistrate has sent up your case directly to the Royal Court. You are to appear before a special session at precisely two-thirty this afternoon, which gives you plenty of time to enjoy a large and expensive lunch. No, please do not ask me to join you. I am feeling a little sick. Good day to you.'

That man was wasted as a policeman: he should have been the headmaster of a High Anglican public school. We slunk out.

The desk sergeant offered no cups of tea this time; he viewed us coldly. He probably knew little of the matter but the scent of opprobrium must have clung to us: we were no longer gents as such but faces to memorize.

He asked me to identify, and sign for, my tape-recorder complete with one cassette. I did so.

'There's nothing on the cassette,' he explained.

'D'you want to bet?' I asked.

My car was triumphantly displaying a parking-ticket, which the others gazed at with moody satisfaction.

'Well, where are we lunching?' asked George.

'At the nearest rookery for me,' I said, 'it is my day for eating crow.'

In the event we were lucky enough to secure a table at the Borsalino, but we could do scant justice to the excellent fare.

'Don't you *like* the Poulet Borsalino?' asked a puzzled proprietor.

Sam looked at him with dreary eyes.

'The Poulet Borsalino is excellent. It is *us* we don't like.'

There was nothing in that for the proprietor; he stole away. (When I tell you that Poulet Borsalino is breast of chicken rolled around gobs of Camembert cheese and deep-fried, you will realize what depths of chagrin caused us to spurn it.)

The Royal Court was intimidating beyond belief. George and Sam's Advocates and my jolly Solicitor joined us in the lobby. The Advocates pursed their lips; Solly gave me a wink. Taking his point, I wrenched the knot of my necktie tight and slid it to one side, rumpling the collar; a simple ruse which reduces one's apparent income by several hundred pounds. *Verb. sap.*, not to mention *experto crede*. We mounted flight after flight of linoleumclad stairs, designed, no doubt, in ancient times to ensure that prisoners arrived in Court flushed and sweating with guilt. Solly goosed me on the stairs, no doubt to cheer me up. Outside the court room itself we were surrendered to the *Greffier*: a terrifying personage in a black robe who looked as though he believed in capital punishment for motoring offences. Soon we were joined by the *Vécomte* – pronounced Viscount – another black-robed officer bearing a great mace, and we processed through oaken doors into the Court. It is a tall, airy, well-lit chamber of great beauty, hung with excellent pictures. Before us, in some majesty and under a splendid canopy, sat the arbiters of our fate. In the centre (Solly explained to me in a whisper) the Deputy Bailiff; to his right a lower throne – empty – where Her Majesty's Lieutenant-Governor would have been sitting had he chosen to exercise his right to attend; on the other side a brace of *Jurats*, chosen from the flower of Jersey's ancient aristocracy. They looked wise and useful, which I believe is their function.

The *Vécomte* stood the mace in its socket before the Bench, the *Greffier* took his stall and the Court of the Inferior Number (so called when only two *Jurats* are sitting) was in session.

The public benches were almost empty: the notice had been too short for the mass of sensation-seekers and only the usual handful of ghoulish old ladies sucking peppermints was there – the ones who don't like all that violence on television and prefer to hear it at first hand, hot from the sty. The sole occupant of the Press bench was my friend Miss H. Glossop, radiating intelligence and goodwill. I had the impression that she would have liked to give me a friendly wave.

There was a deathly hush in the Court, then people recited things in ancient Norman-French; lesser officers repeated them in English; policemen, both Paid and Honorary, related how they had proceeded from one place to another in the execution of their duty and acting on information received and what was more they had notebooks to prove it. Sam's advocate rose and moaned piteously; George's man boomed capably; Solly – a Solly I had never seen before – craved the Court's indulgence to explain briefly that I was – although not in just those words – merely a fucking idiot and more to be pitied than censured.

There was another deathly hush, broken only by peppermint noises from the old ladies. The Deputy Bailiff and *Jurats* retired to debate the finer points and I had a quick consultation with my pocket-flask.

Our judges returned after a very few minutes, wearing damned disinheriting countenances. When everyone was seated, we miscreants were bidden to stand up again. The Deputy Bailiff had a fine command of the language; as he summarized our follies we shrank in stature quite visibly.

Five sonorous minutes made it clear to us, and to all beholders, that we were the sort of reprobates without which the fair Isle of Jersey could well do; that much of the hooliganism, drunkenness and general lowering of moral standards on the Island was directly attributable to such as we; that men of our age should be giving an example to the younger generation and that it had better not happen again, or else.

He took a pause for breath.

'Charlie Strafford Van Cleef Mortdecai,' he said in a voice of doom. 'You are deemed guilty on all three counts. What say you in answer?'

I caught the compelling eye of the old lady opposite. She was leaning forward, her mouth ajar, the great striped peppermint inside clearly visible.

'I'm awfully sorry,' I told the peppermint; 'foolish, ill-advised, unforgivable. Yes. Sorry. Very.'

He told me that I was a man of good family; that I had acted in a disinterested way on my friends' behalf, although foolishly; that the Court was satisfied with my expressions of regret, that the disgrace was probably punishment enough and that the Court was therefore disposed to be lenient. I hung my head to hide my smirk.

'You are therefore committed to prison for a total of twenty-seven months.' The old lady's dentures snapped shut on the unlucky peppermint. 'Or to pay an aggregate fine of four hundred and fifty pounds. Give the prisoner a chair, officer. You are also bound over to be of good behaviour for five years in your own recognizance of a further five hundred pounds.'

He slid his spectacles six inches down his splendid nose. 'Can you pay?' he asked in a kinder voice.

Sam drew fifty pounds less in fines but he didn't get the bit about being of good family, which must have stung.

George drew the same as Sam because, as the Deputy Bailiff pointed out, he had a fine military record. He was on the point of sitting down when the Deputy Bailiff, displaying a sense of timing that Mohammed Ali would have envied, hit him with another hundred and fifty quid for the motor-insurance offence.

Outside, in Royal Square, Solly congratulated me.

'You did very well. I was proud of you. And the Deputy Bailiff was very gentle.'

'*Gentle?*'

'Lord, yes. You should hear him telling off one of us lawyers if we put a foot wrong. Makes one feel like a Labour MP caught soliciting in a public lavatory. Which reminds me, what does one do with a toad?'

'A toad?' I squeaked.

'Well, it could be a frog, I suppose. Sort of brown, warty thing.'

'That's a toad.'

'Yes, well, it arrived this morning and my secretary can't get it to eat. Offered it bread and jam, all sorts of things. Fussy little beast.'

'When you say "arrived" . . .?'

'In a cigar-box. Also enclosed was a piece of lavatory paper, inscribed with the word "Mortdecai". Er, it was *used* lavatory paper.'

I became glad that I had eaten so sparingly at luncheon. Pulling myself together, I said:

'A ribald pun, simply, I should think. On the word *crapaud*, you see.'

'I see,' he said; but he gave me an odd look.

Sam and I dined early, at George's house, then made our selection of women to be protected that night and started to place telephone calls. We were quite unprepared for the stiff hostility with which our suggestions were met; we were, it seemed, social lepers. The first two people we spoke to said, with no attempt at plausibility, that they were otherwise engaged; the third put the receiver down in a marked manner as soon as she heard our names; the fourth said that her husband could look after her perfectly adequately, thank you very much; the fifth said that if we telephoned again she would inform the police. Only the last, a gin-sodden, lust-crazed poetess welcomed our proposal – and her tones made it clear that she had it in mind to do a bit of raping on her own account.

We looked at each other blankly. The telephone rang.

'It's for you, Charlie. Johanna.'

'Charlie,' she said in honeyed tones, 'you may care to know that my bridge-party tonight is off. Yes, off. Lady Pickersgill has telephoned to say that she has a bad cold. So has Lady Cortances. So has Mrs ffrench-Partridge. I hope you are proud of yourself.'

'Gosh, Johanna, I can't tell you how sorry . . .'

'I have just telephoned the airport; they tell me that there are no planes leaving for London tonight. Moreover, the cleaning lady has just told me that she can no longer oblige: she must devote herself in future to caring for her old mother. Whose funeral she attended last year. Moreover, there is a television van parked in the road outside. Moreover, have you seen the evening paper?' Without waiting for a Yes, No, or Don't Know, she hung up.

I went out in the rain to the gate and collected the newspaper. (Your free-born Jersey tradesman will do much for you but he scorns the act of putting newspapers into letterboxes, isn't that odd?)

We studied the front page. The *Jersey Evening Post* had been fair, nay, kindly to us in the report of the trial but the photograph taken of us on the pavement outside the Court was unfortunate to say the least. We three shambling offenders huddled guiltily together, surrounded by venal shysters, mopping and mowing. George was glaring at the camera in a way that could only be called homicidal; Sam looked like an expletive deleted from a Watergate tape while I had been caught scratching my behind and sniggering over my shoulder. All most unfortunate.

We looked at each other; or to be exact, they looked at me while I shiftily avoided their eyes.

'I know,' I said brightly, 'let's all get drunk!'

They stopped looking at me and looked at each other. Sonia reappeared, looked at the photograph and promptly got a fit of the giggles. This can be quite becoming in some women but Sonia has never learned the art: her version is too noisy and she tends to fall about on sofas and things, displaying her knickers. Where applicable. George made his displeasure clear to her and she went back to the real love of her life – her washing-up machine; nasty, noisy thing.

Sam and George started to re-enact the 'let's all look at Charlie in a hateful way' scene, so I rose. I can be hurt, you know.

'I am going home to watch the television,' I said stiffly.

'Oh no you're not,' snapped George. 'You're going home to change into dark clothes, soft shoes and a weapon, and you're reporting back here in fifteen minutes with Jock, similarly clad.'

Now, I may choose to make myself seem a bit of a craven at times, when it suits my book, but I don't take crap like that – even from retired brigadiers. *Especially* from retired brigadiers. I turned to him and gave him a slow, insubordinate stare.

'It will take *twenty* minutes at least,' I said insubordinately, 'because, things at home being what they are, I shall have to look out the clothes myself.'

'Do your best,' said George, not unkindly.

In the event, I was back there in twenty-eight minutes.

'Right,' said George. 'Here's the plan. Since these idiots will not let us lie up *in* their houses we shall have to patrol *outside* their houses – from now until midnight. I shall move between Hautes Croix and this house; Jock will drop Sam at La Sergenté from where he will make his way to St Magloire's Manor and so, past Canberra House, back here; Jock himself, since both Sonia and Johanna are alone and unguarded, will work between Wutherings and Les Cherche-fuites; you, Charlie, will cover the lanes between here and Belle Etoile Bay. None of us will use metalled roads. Any questions?'

There weren't any questions.

15

There the gladiator, pale for thy pleasure,
Drew bitter and perilous breath;
There torments laid hold on the treasure
Of limbs too delicious for death;
When thy gardens were lit with live torches;
When the world was a steed for thy rein;
When the nations lay prone in thy porches,
Our Lady of Pain.

Dolores

A cold coming I had of it, I don't mind telling you, just the worst time of the year for a vigilante patrol. I believe I've already given you my views about the month of May in the British Isles. This May night, as I picked my glum way down to Belle Etoile Bay, was cold and black as a schoolgirl's heart and the moon – in its last quarter and now quite devoid of the spirit of public service – reminded me only of a Maria Teresa silver dollar which I had once seen clenched between the buttocks of a Somali lady who was, I fancy, no better than she should be. But enough of that.

Down I stole to Belle Etoile Bay. The sea breathed hoarsely, like a rapist out of training. Back I stole, breathing like a middle-aged vigilante who has neither pocket-flask nor sandwich-case about him because his wife isn't speaking to him. As I entered Chestnut Lane (*La Rue des Châtaigniers*), nearing the end of my beat for the first time round, a *châtaignier* or chestnut tree quietly divided itself into two *châtagniers* or chestnut trees and one of the component parts drifted in my direction. I am often asked what to do when things of this kind happen to you and I always divided my advice into several alternative parts; viz, either

a. blubber, or

b. run, or

c. drop on to your marrow-bones and beg for mercy.

If, of course, you belonged, as I did, to an absurd Special Something Unit in the war – yes, that 1939–45 one – then you can do better. What I did was to drop silently to the ground and roll over several times. This accomplished, I plucked out my pistol and waited. The tree-person froze. After a long time he spoke.

'I can't see your face,' he said, 'but I can see your great arse. I'm putting a Lüger bullet into it in about three seconds flat unless you gimme a good reason why not.'

I stood up, coaxing my lungs back into service.

'Jock,' I said, 'I am recommending you for the Woodcraft Medal. Your impersonation of a tree was most plausible.'

' 'Ullo, Mr Charlie.'

'What do you have on your person, apart from that machine-pistol which I have repeatedly told you not to carry?'

'Got a flat half-bottle of brown rum.'

'Faugh,' I said. 'I'm not as thirsty as that. When you are next at the Wutherings end of your beat, be so good as to find and fill my pocket-flask; I shall patrol back to Belle Etoile Bay and meet you here again in, say, thirty minutes.'

'Right, Mr Charlie. I dare say you'd like the sandwich-case, too?'

'Very well, Jock, since you insist. I suppose I should keep my strength up.'

'Right, Mr Charlie.' He started to melt away.

'Jock!'

'Yeah?'

'There should be a few scraps of cold pheasant in the fridge.'

'They're still there; I don't like pheasant, do I?'

'They will do for the sandwiches, but at all costs remember: pheasant sandwiches are made with brown bread.'

'Yeah.'

He went on melting away, as I did.

Melting away from Chestnut Lane to Belle Etoile Bay involves getting lost, muddy and wet; not to mention breaking your shins against nameless bits of farm machinery left around *on purpose* by Jerseymen. When I got to the Bay the sea was making the same sort of hoarse, defeated noise: 'Oh gaw-blimey,' it seemed to be moaning, " 'ow much longer 'ave I gotter go on wiv this meaningless to-ing and fro-ing?'

'I couldn't have put it better myself,' I assured it.

I turned back towards Chestnut Lane: unlike the sea, I could look forward to pocket-flasks and sandwich-cases. That was my error: the gods keep a sharp and jealous eye on chaps who hug themselves in such expectations.

Bursting cheerfully through a hedgerow, I saw a large and tree-like shape in front of me. I thought it was Jock.

'Jock?' I said.

The shape took a tree-like pace towards me and hit me very hard on the temple. I fell, more slowly than you could imagine, to the ground, my face smacking the mud as gratefully as though it were a pillow. I was incapable of movement but not really unconscious. A small flashlight was turned on to me; I shut my tortured eyes against it but not before I had noticed a shoe close to my face. It was a *good* shoe, the sort of heavy, tan walking-shoe that I might have bought from Ducker's of Oxford in the days when my father paid my bills.

The light went out. I felt a hand feeling my temple in a knowledgeable sort of way; it hurt damnably but there was no crepitation – I dared to hope that I might live. Then two strong hands lifted me to a kneeling position and I opened my eyes. Towering above me was a horrendous creature with a face such as hell itself would have rejected. It was near enough for me to receive its stench, which was abominable. Then its knee came up and struck the point of my jaw with a deafening, blinding smash.

Dimly-experienced things happened to me in my stupor; I was rummaged and buffeted, hoisted and wrenched. Wisely, I decided to remain asleep, and sleep I did until an excruciating pain screamed out of my right ear. I jerked wildly from the pain, which redoubled it, so I fainted, only to awake instantly with an even sharper agony. A great explosion happened close to the ear – and more pain. Awake now, in a sort of way, I mustered enough sense to remain motionless while my frightful assailant rustled away. When I was sure that he had gone I delicately explored my situation. I found that I was standing against a tree. My hands and feet were unencumbered. I tried moving my head – and screamed. Infinitely gently I raised my hands to my ear, asking them to tell my scrambled brain what it was all about. When my hands told me, I fainted again – just as you would have – and awoke instantly with another scream of pain.

My ear, you see, had been nailed to the tree.

I stood very still for what seemed an hour. Then I reached behind me and drew out the Banker's Special pistol from my hip-pocket. I filled my lungs and opened my mouth to shout for help but a sharp agony came from my jawbone and a horrid grating noise and my tongue discovered that my teeth were all in the wrong places.

I pointed the pistol into the air and squeezed the trigger but I had not the strength to work the double-action. Using both hands I contrived to cock the hammer, then I fired. Then again. Then, with immense difficulty, once more. Jock had often acted as loader for me in the shooting field and he would recognize the three-shots distress-signal.

I waited for an eternity. I dared not spend any more cartridges on signals: I needed them in case the madman came back. I spent the time trying to keep awake – each time I started to fade out my weight came on the ear with excruciating effect – and in trying to remember whether it was Lobengula or Cetewayo who used to nail minor offenders to trees. They had to tear *themselves* loose, you see, before the hyenas got them.

At last I heard a bellow from Jock, the most welcome bellow of my life. I croaked an answer. The bellow came nearer. When Jock finally loomed up before me I levelled the pistol at his belly. An hour before, I would have trusted him with my life but tonight the world was insane. All I could think of was that I was not going to be hurt any more. He stepped closer. I sniffed hungrily. There was no trace of the loathly stench of the witch.

'You all right, Mr Charlie?' he asked.

'Eye aws ogen,' I explained.

'Eh?'

'Aw ogen,' I explained crossly, pointing to my chin.

'Jaw broken. Lumme, so it is.'

'Ailed oo ee,' I added, pointing to my ear.

He struck a match and hissed with distress when he saw the plight I was in. The nail, it seems, had been driven in to its very head; my ear had puffed up around it and was full of blood.

'I don't reckon I could get a claw-hammer under it, Mr Charlie. Think I'll have to cut it.'

I didn't want to know what he was going to do: I just wanted him to do it, so that I could lie down and get to sleep. I made vigorous motions towards the ear and shut my eyes hard.

I couldn't grit my teeth while he cut a channel from the head of the nail to the edge of my ear, because my teeth wouldn't meet but I remember weeping copiously. He asked me to move my head. No good: the bit of gristle under the head of the nail held fast. There was a long pause then, to my horror, I felt the point of his knife against the corner of my eye. I wrenched away convulsively and screamed as the ear came free.

'Sorry, Mr Charlie,' he said as he gathered me up from the kindly mud.

The next time I woke up, Jock was dragging me out of the car and into the Emergency part of the General Hospital in St Helier. He propped me up against the counter, where a kindly but stern lady was making tut-tutting noises at me. She handed Jock a form to fill in: I snatched it and scrawled 'SEE IF JOHANNA OK'. Jock nodded, lowered me to the floor and vanished.

The time after that, I awoke under a fierce white light and a compassionate black face. The latter seemed to belong to a Pakistani doctor who was doing fine embroidery on my ear. He beamed at me.

'Werry nasty accident,' he assured me. 'You may thank lucky stars you are in land of living.'

I started to open my mouth to say something witty about Peter Sellers but found that I couldn't. Open my mouth, I mean. It was all sort of wired up and my tongue seemed to be trapped in a barbed-wire entanglement.

'Please to keep quite still,' said the nice doctor, 'and you will be as new in twinkling of eye. If not, all my good work is gone for Burton.'

I kept still.

'Nurse,' he called over his shoulder, 'patient is now on surface.'

The stern lady from Casualty Reception appeared, waving forms.

'Just name, address and next of kin will do for now,' she said, not too sternly. I lifted a pen weighing a hundredweight and wrote. She went away. A moment later she was back, whispering to the doctor.

'Mr Mortdecai,' he said to me, 'it seems we have just admitted a lady of the same name: is she with you? Mrs Johanna Mortdecai?'

I started to get up; they held me down. I fought them. Someone put a needle in my arm and told me gently that the doctor seeing to Johanna would come to see me presently. Unwillingly, I passed out.

When next I awoke I was in a warm, tight bed and a warm, scratchy nightshirt which was soaked with sweat. I felt like hell and a thousand hangovers: death seemed infinitely desirable. Then I remembered Johanna and started to get up but a little, thin nurse held me down without effort, as though she were smoothing a sheet. A new face appeared, a large, pale chap.

'Mr Mortdecai?' he said. 'Good morning. I'm the doctor who has been attending to your wife. She's going to be all right but she's rather badly torn and has lost a good deal of blood.'

I made frantic writing gestures and he handed me a pen and a pad.

'Raped?' I wrote.

'To tell the truth, we don't know. There seems to be no damage down there, although there are extensive injuries elsewhere. We can't ask her about the other thing because she is in deep shock: I'm afraid he hurt her rather badly.'

I took up the pen again.

'Is her ear badly disfigured?' I wrote.

He looked at the words for a long time, as though he couldn't understand them. Slowly he met my eyes, with a look so compassionate that I was frightened.

'I'm sorry, Mr Mortdecai, I thought you knew. Her injuries are not the same as yours at all.'

16

Let us rise up and part; she will not know.
Let us go seaward as the great winds go,
Full of blown sand and foam; what help is here?
There is no help, for all these things are so,
And all the world is bitter as a tear.
And how these things are, though ye strove to show,
She would not know.

A Leave-Taking

The next month or so was pretty rotten. If your mouth is all wired together, you see, you can't brush your teeth and if you also catch a cold, as I did, the whole situation becomes squalid beyond belief. Moreover, they had fitted a beastly tube into one nostril and down into my gullet, and it was through this that they fed me nameless, though probably nourishing, pap. Worse, every book I started to read seemed to carry, on the third or fourth page, wonderfully vivid descriptions of gravy soup, oysters, roasted partridges and steak-and-kidney puddings. Whenever I quaked with lust for food, the little thin nurse would clip a bottle on to my nose-tube and fill my poor stomach with the costive pap, at the same time trying to slip an icy bed-pan under my bottom. Naturally, I never put up with this latter indignity: I used to stride – or perhaps totter – to the loo under my own steam, festooned with protesting nurses and with gruel streaming from my nosetube: an awesome sight I dare say.

146

When I had some strength I found out where Johanna was and used to creep out and visit her. She was pale and looked much older. I couldn't talk and she didn't want to. I would sit on the side of her bed and pat her hand a bit. She would pat mine a bit and we would wink at each other in a wan sort of way. It helped. I arranged through Jock for flowers and grapes and things to be sent to her at frequent intervals and she arranged, through Jock, for me to receive boxes of Sullivan's cigarettes and things like that. The night nurse, who was fat and saucy, contrived to fiddle a straw into my mouth through a gap where a tooth is missing behind my upper left canine; thereafter I was able, each evening, to drink half a bottle of Burgundy, which blunted the edge of misery a little.

The doctors were pleased with my jaw, they said it was mending well but my ear went bad and they had to cut some of it off, and then the rest of it. That was why Johanna was discharged quite a bit earlier than I was.

My homecoming was not jolly; Johanna had known about the ear but she was a bit taken aback when she saw me without it (I'd discharged myself the moment they took the bandages off) and she burst into tears – a thing I'd never seen her do before. I made a few jests about how she had never thought much of my looks anyway and the lop-sided effect might grow on her but she was inconsolable. I shall never understand women. You probably think you do but you're wrong, you know. They're not a bit like us.

In the end I took her gently to bed and we lay there hand in hand in the dark so that she could cry without my seeing her eyes get puffy and we listened to *Le Nozze di Figaro* which turned out to be a bad mistake: one forgets that it's not nearly such a lighthearted piece for people who understand Italian. As Johanna does. When it came to *Dove Sono* she really broke down and wanted to tell me all about what had happened on that dreadful night. This was too much for me, I simply wasn't up to it; I rushed downstairs and fetched a tray of drinks and we both got a little drunk and then it was better, much better; but we both knew that I had let her down. Again. Well, that's the price you pay for being a coward. I only wish one could be told exactly how much the instalments are, and when they are likely to fall due. A moral coward, you see, is simply someone who has read the fine print on the back of his Birth Certificate and seen the little clause which says 'You can't win'. He knows from then on that the smart thing to do is to run away from everything and he does so. But he doesn't have to like it.

'Jock,' I said the next morning. 'Mrs Mortdecai will not be down to breakfast.' I looked at him levelly. He twigged. His good eye crumpled up into a huge wink, which left the glass one – carelessly inserted – leering up at the cornice. Sure enough, he had read my mind and the eggs and bacon, when they arrived, were mounted on delicious fried bread and accompanied by fried potatoes, all quite counter to Johanna's 'Standing Order Concerning Mr Mortdecai's Waistline'. Well, dash it, why should I persecute my waistline; it's never done me any harm. Yet.

The last fried potato had captured the last runlet of egg-yolk and was about to home in on the Mortdecai waistline when George and Sam appeared. They looked grave and friendly for I too, now, had suffered, I was a member of the club – but they both looked askance at the marmalade and richly-buttered toast which Jock brought in at that moment. Sam never breakfasts and George believes that breakfast is something that gentlemen eat at a quarter past dawn, not at half-past noon.

I waved them to chairs and offered them richly-buttered toast and marmalade. They glanced at it with ill-concealed longing but refused: they were strong; *strong*.

I knew most of their news: there had been only two rapes in the intervening period and one of those had been a bit suspect: a young Jersey girl who was already a teeny bit pregnant by a fiancé who had absent-mindedly joined a boat going to Australia. The other incident bore all the marks of being 'one of ours' but the victim was a hopeless witness, even by female standards, and could add nothing to our dossier.

George and Sam had been patrolling in a desultory and half-hearted way but with no results except that Sam said he had chased a mackintoshed suspect for half a mile but had lost him in the outbuildings of one of George's tenant-farmers. A search had produced nothing but a pair of bicycle-clips in a disused cow-stable.

Sonia was quite recovered. Violet was much worse: clearly catatonic now, having to be watched night and day.

George was withdrawn and morose; Sam was in a state of suppressed hysteria which I found disturbing: long silences punctuated by random and bitter witticisms of poor quality. Not at all the Sam I had known and loved.

News exhausted, we looked at one another dully.

'Drinks?' I asked, dully.

George looked at his wristwatch; Sam opened his mouth and shut it again. I poured drinks. We drank three each, although we had had no luncheon. Johanna joined us. By the hard light of noon she looked older by ten years but her air of command was still there.

'Well, have you boys made a plan?' she asked, looking at me, bless her.

We made three apologetic grimaces. Sam started to sketch out a smile but gave up at the attempt. George cleared his throat. We looked at him wearily.

'Let's go fishing,' he said. 'My bass-boat's all new-painted and varnished and they're putting it into the water tomorrow. Do us all good, a bit of a sail. Try for some mackerel, eh?'

Sam and I, by our silences, registered total disapprobation. George on land is merely brigadier-like; at sea his mission seems to be to prove that Captain Bligh was a softy.

'Oh yes, Charlie, do go!' cried Johanna. 'A bit of a sail will do you so much good, and I would adore some fresh mackerels.'

I shifted sulkily in my chair.

'Or pollocks,' she added, 'or basses or breams. *Please*, Charlie?'

'Oh, very well,' I said. 'If Sam's coming.'

'Of course,' said Sam bitterly, 'of course, of *course*.'

'Wonderful!' said Johanna.

'Nine o'clock, then?' said George.

'Dark by that time,' I said.

'Got a dinner engagement at eight,' said Sam.

'I meant nine a.m.' said George.

We stared at him. Finally he settled for immediately after luncheon and, later still, agreed that this should be construed as 2.30 p.m.

By an excess of zeal, I was at Ouaisné Bay at three minutes short of 2.30 p.m. Clearly, the thing to do was look in at the pub on the shore and seek a fortifying drop of this and that. Sam was already there, fortifying himself diligently.

We grunted, then sat for a while in a silence broken only by the steady sip-sipping noise of two born landsmen about to embark on a sixteen-foot boat captained by another landsman with a Nelson-complex. George stamped into the bar and stared rudely at us.

'Hullo, sailor!' we cried in unison. We had not expected him to smile, so we were not disappointed.

'Waiting for you for five minutes,' he said. 'Can you tear yourselves away? Got any dunnage?'

Sam's dunnage consisted of a slim volume of verse wrapped in a plastic bag to keep typhoons out. Mine was a sou-wester and full oilskins (because the meteorologists had predicted calm, sunny weather), one flask each of hot soup, hot coffee and the cheaper sort of Scotch whisky, my sandwich-case and a pot of cold curried potatoes in case of shipwreck or other Acts of God. George carried a battered, professional-looking ditty-bag full, no doubt, of *sensible* things.

The boat, I must say, looked splendid in all its beginning-of-season paint and varnish and carried a huge, new outboard motor. George's ubiquitous Plumber, who also acts as his waterman, helped us to launch; the new motor started without trouble and we sailed away across little dancing blue waves which stirred even my black heart. There was a light haze which was probably thicker further out, for the doomily-named *La Corbière* ('The Place of Ravens' – our friendly neighbourhood lighthouse) was giving out its long, grunting moan every three minutes, like a fat old person straining at the seat. We recked not of it. In no time we were the best part of a mile out and George bade us troll our lines for mackerel. We trolled, if that is the word I want, for half an hour, but to no avail.

Puffins, shags and smews passed overhead, puffing and shagging and doing whatever smews do, but they weren't interested in that bit of water. Moreover, there were no gulls feeding, and no gulls means no fry and no fry means no mackerel.

'There are no mackerel here, George,' I said, 'moreover, we are going too fast for mackerel; two or three knots would be better.'

'Nonsense,' he replied.

I kneaded a piece of Marmite sandwich and a piece of cheese ditto into a lump on a larger hook, added a heavier weight to my line and almost at once boated a fine big pollock. George glared. I slipped Sam a lum of my mixture and soon he, too, had a good pollock.

'Keep it up, George,' I said, 'this is the perfect speed for pollock.'

'Mackerel obviously not in yet,' he grated. 'Going to bear in a bit, find some broken water and try for bass.'

La Corbière groaned, muffling deeper groans from Sam and me. There's nothing we like better than broken water, of course, but we prefer to brave it with a professional boatman at the helm. In we went, though, and found a stretch of the stuff which looked as though it might serve, although it was unpleasantly close to a razor-edged miniature cliff at the shoreline. Worse was to come.

'Going to step the mast,' said George; 'run up a scrap of sail, then we can cut this engine, get a bit of quiet.'

I am nothing of a mariner but this appalled me. I looked at Sam. He looked at me.

'George,' said Sam gently, 'are you certain that's wise? I mean, isn't this a lee-shore or something?'

'Rubbish,' he said. 'A shore is only a lee-shore if there's an on-shore wind. There is no wind at present but at this time of a warm day we can depend upon some light off-shore airs. And I must remind you, Sam, that there can only be one skipper in a boat: disputing an order can *kill* people.'

'Aye, aye,' said Sam, in a puzzled, insubordinate voice.

I started to remember that I hadn't heard *La Corbière* for some minutes, wondered whether a breeze had got up to dissipate the haze, but too late now. George had raised and locked the little mast into its tabernacle and was halfway up it, wrestling with the daft little leg-o'-mutton sail, when the first gust out of the South-East hit us.

Over we went on to our beam-ends, the outboard motor screaming as the screw found no water to bite, George dangling then vanishing overside amidst a raffle of canvas and cordage. In we drove to the murderous rock, beam on, until a fearful gnashing noise told us that the mast had gone and we felt our craft strike – not with a crash but a nasty, mushy sensation. Bubbles came up from where George must be. I seized an oar and fended us off as best I could; Sam grabbed the gutting-knife and slashed and hacked us free from the raffle of wreckage overside. We caught one glimpse of George, face up, an arm flailing, then the undertow seemed to catch him and he vanished under the boat. He reappeared after a minute, twenty feet to seaward, still with one arm thrashing the water; we ground against the rocks again and again. I fended us off with one oar. The motor coughed and died. Like the fools we were, none of us was wearing a life-jacket, nor was there visible a length of casting-line to throw to George. As I battled with the oar Sam crawled to the little forepeak and rummaged frantically, dragging out our dunnage in search of anything useful; then kneeling, frozen, staring at what he had ripped out of George's sea-bag. It was a tight ball of cloth, wrapped about with ¼" line. Sam raised this to his nose and made a face of loathing.

'What the hell are you doing?' I screamed against the rising noise of wind and sea. He didn't answer. He undid the parcel: it was a mackintosh, the cuffs and shoulders studded with nails. From it he drew a hideous rubber mask. He didn't look at me; he wiped his fingers on a thwart and looked to where George had thrashed his way, one-armed, almost to the side of the boat. Sam took the other oar and slowly, as though carrying out some ritual gesture, raised it two-handed high above his head, blade upwards.

George had his good hand on the gunwale now and we could see a great flap of skin hanging from his scalp and the bloody ruin of his crushed arm. He looked at Sam. His hand left the gunwale and his face vanished. Sam threw the oar into the boat, then lurched aft to the motor. I fended off for dear life: our timbers couldn't take much more punishment from those granite daggers. The engine roared into life; Sam revved it until it screamed and then suddenly we were in open water. I started to bail. Once, looking over my shoulder, I thought I saw something half a furlong away with an arm up-raised, but it was probably only a cormorant.

We were in sight of Ouaisné Bay before either of us said a word.

'I suppose he must be dead by now?'

I didn't answer: it hadn't really been a question. And I was thinking.

'Sonia wasn't raped,' I said flatly.

'No. We'd been lovers – if that's a word fit to use – for months. First time was an accident, both drunk at a party. After that she made me do it again and again; swore she'd tell George if I didn't. That first day of all this, when you and George came home unexpectedly, we thought we were caught and I told Sonia to yell "rape" while I got out of the window. She'd been reading all that muck about the Beast of Jersey, that's what put all the witchcraft trimmings into her head.'

'But George worked it out. What he did to Violet was revenge, simply?'

'Yes. Perhaps he was telling us that he knew. I should have realized. Suppose I was too upset to think it through.'

'I see. Then he must have got a sort of taste for it, I suppose. Brought out a streak of insanity in him, perhaps?'

'An officer and gentleman,' said Sam. He made it sound like the punch-line of a vile joke.

I finished bailing and tied George's horrid paraphernalia to the spare anchor and threw it over the side. I didn't care whether someone might fish it up, I just wanted it out of my sight.

The Plumber met us on the beach, helped us haul-up on to the trailer.

'Where's Mr Breakspear, then?'

'Lost overside. We were nearly wrecked. Tell the Coast-guard, would you.'

'My Chri',' said the Plumber. Then, 'Oh, there's a phone call at the pub for Mr Davenant, from England, urgent. You have to ask for the Personal Calls Operator.' Sam started to walk towards the pub, then broke into a shambling run.

'So it was Mr Breakspear all the time,' said the Plumber.

I didn't answer. I was wondering how many people had known all the time. Perhaps I should have asked my gardener. Perhaps he would even have told me.

Sam came out of the pub, bleak-faced.

'Violet has killed herself,' he said carefully. 'Let's go home. Things to do.'

'Have to go to the police first,' I said. 'Report George missing.'

'Yes, of course. I'd forgotten about that.' His voice was gentle now.

'Don't you want your fish?' the Plumber called after us.

'No, thanks,' I said. 'We know where they've been.'

It was dark when we left the Police Station and drove up the *Grande Route de S. Jean* towards our homes.

'Want to talk?' I asked diffidently.

'Vi was left alone for a moment – nurse went to the loo – and she just got out of bed and hurled herself through the closed window. Can't blame the nurse; Vi hadn't stirred for days. They warned me, of course. Catatonics think they can fly, you see. Angels.'

'Sam –' I started.

'Please shut up, Charlie.'

I tried again when we got to his house.

'Look,' I said, 'won't you please stay with us tonight?'

'Good night, Charlie,' he said and shut the door.

At home, I told Johanna about things as briefly as I could, then announced that I wanted to write letters. I went up to my dressing-room and stood at the open window, in the dark. Across the fields Sam's house was a blaze of lights, then, one by one, they started to go out. I gripped the window-sill. It was very cold and a thin rain sifted on to my face.

When the shot came I stayed where I was.

Jock drifted into the room.

'Shot from over Cherche-fuites way,' he said.

'Yes,' I said.

'Heavy-calibre pistol, by the sound of it.'

'That's right.'

'Well, are we going over there?'

'No.'

'You going to phone then, Mr Charlie?'

'Get out, Jock.'

Five minutes later Johanna crept in and took one of my arms in both of hers, pressing it to her poor breast.

'Dear Charlie, why are you standing here in the dark and shivering. And *crying*? All right, I'm sorry, I'm sorry, of course you're not crying, I can see you're not.'

But she closed the window and drew the curtains and led me to my bed, making me lie down, spreading a quilt over me.

'Good night, Charlie,' she said. 'Please sleep now.'

'Oh, very well,' I said. But I would have liked to tell her about it.

'Johanna,' I said, as she opened the door.

'Yes, Charlie?'

'I forgot to ask – how is the canary?'

She didn't answer.

'He's dead, isn't he?'

She closed the door, very gently.

Read on for an extract from the next book in the
Charlie Mortdecai series:

The Great Mortdecai Moustache Mystery

Available now in Penguin Books.

I

A pair of knaves for openers

Trust me that honist man is as comen a name as the name of a
good felow, that is to say a dronkerd, a tauerne hanter, a
riotter, a gamer, a waster: so are among the comen sort al men
honist men that are not knowin for manifest naughtye knaues.
—*Sir Thomas Wyatt in a letter to his son*

'I wooden, Mr Charlie, I reelly wooden,' mumbled Jock,
moodily gnashing his toothsome way through the bunch
of grapes he had brought me. 'I mean, you know the aggro
you're going to get if you try to complete that projeck, if
you'll pardon the expression.'

I was, you see, in what Jock calls 'horse-piddle' – what
you and I would call 'King Edward the Fifth's Hospital for
Officers Who Cannot Afford the London Clinic' – and was
recovering from a trifling operation which is none of your
business. (Oh, very well, if you must know, I had been there
to have a cluster of haemorrhoids beheaded, which was one
good reason for having no appetite for grapes. The other
good reason was that I don't happen to like grapes, a fact
well known to Jock.)

Perhaps I should explain that I have a Fully
Comprehensive Accident Protection Policy which
guarantees that if anyone even looks as though he's going
to be horrid to me he will be cured of all known disease.

Permanently. The Policy's name is Jock.

Jock, in short, is my large, dangerous, one-fanged, one-eyed thug: we art-dealers need to keep a thug, you understand, although it isn't always easy to persuade HM's Commissioners for Inland Revenue that it's a necessary expense. Jock is the best thug that money can buy; he's quality all through, slice him where you will. When I decided to conserve my energy resources – who'd want to become fossil fuel? – and gave up art-dealing in favour of matrimony I tried to pay him off but he just sort of stayed on and took to calling himself a manservant. He is not quite sane and never quite sober but he can still pop out seven streetlights with nine shots from his old Luger while ramming his monstrous motorbike through heavy after-theatre traffic. I've seen him do it. As a matter of fact, I was on the pillion-seat at the time, whimpering promises to God that if He got me home safely I would never tell another lie. God kept His part of the deal, but God isn't an art-dealer, is He? (Don't answer that.)

Ah yes, well, I've introduced both God and Jock so I'd better start tidily by putting on record that my name is The Honble. Charlie Mortdecai. I was actually *christened* Charlie; I suspect that my mother was getting at my father in some unsubtle way, she was like that. He wouldn't have noticed, he wasn't good at jokes.

Yes, well again, there I was, in my valuable hospital bed, tossing back little shots of Chivas Regal from the bottle-cap while Jock tore juicily at the bunch of grapes already cited, which had camouflaged the top of the paper bag in which he had brought me the booze. Pray do not think that Jock had no stomach for the Scotch; he, too, dearly loves such fluids but would have been shocked if I had offered him a suck at the Chivas R., for he knows his station in life. He was, in any case, more concerned to persuade me from the perilous venture upon which I was embarking.

'Honestly, Mr Charlie,' he pleaded on, 'don't do it, I beg of you. It's bloody madness, you know it is.' He paced to the open window, sprayed a moody mouthful of grape-stones into the welkin and returned to my well-smoothed counterpane. 'Playing with bleeding fire, that's what you're doing, Mr Charlie.'

'Enough, Jock!' I commanded, raising a commanding head. 'I am touched by your concern for my personal safety but my mind is made up. I shall go through with this, come what may. I must strike a blow for the free world while I still have my strength.' My commanding hand strayed to the subject of our debate: the already thriving thicket of vegetation which sprouted from the Mortdecai upper lip.

My ravishing wife, Johanna, you see, had taken the opportunity of my hospitalisation to nip across the Atlantic Ocean and pay a call on her terrifying old mama, the Gräfin or gryphon Grettheim and I too had seized an opportunity; viz., to grow a moustache, thus filling a much-needed gap between the southern end of the nose and the northern ditto of the mouth. It was prospering well although it tickled a bit – indeed, no fewer than two of the nurses had assured me that it tickled quite deliciously. I had often longed for such a thing – yes, the moustache – and was devoting all my energies to it. Meditation and a high-protein diet work best, you may take my word for it.

'Well, Mr Charlie, I daresay you know best,' said Jock in glum tones which belied his words, 'but I wooden be in your shoes for anythink when Madam gets back.' With that he pulled the now stripped stalk of the grape-bunch from his pursed lips, looking for all the world like some conjurer extracting a small Christmas tree from a rabbit's backside, and rose gloomily to his great feet. I raised a brace of benign fingers and promised that no blame would attach to him; I would assure Johanna that he had fought the good fight.

'By the way, Jock, was it you who kindly bought those delicious grapes for me?'

'Yeah. 'Course. Well, I put them on your account at Fortnum's, didden I? They weren't half expensive. Very tasty though.'

'Yes. They *sounded* tasty indeed.'

'Well, I got to go, Mr Charlie, got a mate coming round to play dominoes.'

'Splendid, it will keep you off the streets. Enjoy yourself.

Having any trouble with the new lock on the liquor-cupboard?'

He left in a huffed sort of way. I fished out the pocket-mirror to see what progress the moustache had made since lunch-time, then rang for a nurse.

———·—·—·—·—·———

During my last few days in hospital nothing much happened. Jock continued to smuggle in my whisky-ration; young nurses sneaked into my room for a tot when the senior nurses weren't administering shaming enemas; the Senior Consultant – a chum of mine – popped into the room to scrounge a tot himself (poor underpaid wretch, he probably had to drink cooking-sherry at home) and to urge me to give up drinking and smoking lest I should contract Art-Dealer's Elbow; birds jabbered outside the window at dawn (when do the bloody things *sleep*?); and colour television made the evenings hideous. I applied for permission to have my canary brought in but it was rated a health-hazard, so my studious brain applied itself to nurse-watching. I soon had them scientifically classified by plumage, habitat and ethology, as follows: the elderly, ugly ones in moult, whose only pleasure was the administration of cruel enemas to the root of the trouble, so to say, and who sniffed like aunts when they caught a whiff of whisky on my breath; the Roman Catholic ones whose characteristic cry was 'You may stop that at once or I'll tell Sister;' the very brightly-plumaged ones who chirruped 'Ooh, you are awful;' and the almost-pretty ones who only said 'Oooh!'

Time passed slowly and my moustache inched forth so languidly that I sometimes feared that it was losing its sense of purpose in life – but there came a day when certain tubes were uncoupled from undignified bits of the Mortdecai chassis and I was told that I might navigate to the lav under my own steam. As I tottered thither in an imperious dressing-gown I could not but notice an uncommon number of junior nurses loitering in the corridor and, it seemed to me, suppressing maidenly titters. A few minutes later I realised why.

Whimpering, I was helped back to bed while squadrons of ward-maids, helpless with happy laughter, moved into the lav with mops and buckets. Later – much later – I felt proud to have brought a little sunshine into the drab lives of those underpaid little angels of mercy; but for the time being I sulked.

Soon, though, all wounds were healed and I received my Honourable Discharge from the very Matron herself; she said, pronouncing the capital letters sonorously, that I had made a Splendid Recovery and that she heard On All Sides that I had been a Good Patient. She also hoped that I had Learnt my Lesson and would not, in future, come into contact with Damp Grass, which she assured me was the ætiology of the common or garden haemorrhoid. I started to explain that, if she was right, then the piles would have manifested themselves on my knees and elbows, but she gave me an Odd Look. I suspected that she was just hanging about in the hope of a handsome tip but I'm sure you can't tip Matrons less than a tenner, and in any case I knew that she probably owned shares in the lazar-houses and would get her slice from the dripping roast as soon as I had paid my bill, so I stayed my generous hand.

Jock had a swansdown cushion waiting for me in the Rolls – he had a wonderful grasp of the fundamental necessities of life, bless him.

II

A queen, a one-eyed jack and a wild card

They flee from me that sometime did me seek
With naked foot stalking in my chamber,
I have seen them gentle tame and meek
That now are wild and do not remember
That sometime they put themselves in danger
To take bread at my hand; and now they range
Busily seeking with a continual change.

Back at the Mortdecai half-mansion in the North of the Island – sorry, I thought you knew I lived in Jersey, Channel Islands – I was convalescing splendidly, mounted on cushionry of the finest and downiest, kneading Pomade Hongroise into the fruiting vineyard of my upper lip and applying a little Cognac internally, when the door flew open and a radiant Johanna (to wit, my wife) burst into the room and sprang rapturously into my arms, uttering many a glad cry – only to recoil instantly, giving bent to one of those shrieks which only the gently-nurtured can command and then only when they find their mouths full of well-pomaded moustache. I have never quite known what the word 'eldritch' means but there is no reasonable doubt in my mind that eldritch is what that shriek was. No Sabine woman would have got into the quarter-finals that afternoon.

There followed what I can only call an Ugly Scene. She began temperately enough by saying that the Surgeon

General of the USA had specifically warned the public against such defilements and that he could call on the support of most of the sterner prophets in the Old Testament. I put it to her logically that whereas I had freely given her my heart, soul, other assorted organs and all my worldly goods, I had never put anything in writing about my upper lip, had I? This reasonable argument did not sway her at all – women use a different logic from men, you must have noticed that – and she redoubled her Jeremiad, calling my lip-valance a social disease and drawing impassioned parallels with the Watergate cover-up.

Thinking to silence her into melting, wifely submission I swept her masterfully into my arms. This time it was my turn to recoil with the eldritch shriek as she smartened me up with a gently-nurtured knee in the groin. 'Don't you dare to point that thing at me,' she snarled and, 'If I ever wish to munch half-grown brambles I shall go and graze in Potter's Field,' and again, 'Go mingle with the pimps in the Place Pigalle, your face looks like a dirty postcard,' and, 'You look as though you were going down on an alley-cat.' Soon afterwards, bitter words were being exchanged. Finally she clicked open the diamond-studded cover of her Patek Philippe watch and said coldly, 'As of this moment you have precisely five minutes in which to shave yourself back into the ecology.'

I was not going to take that sort of thing from any mere sex-object, least of all the wife of my personal bosom; I folded my arms lordlily and favoured the ceiling with a stony stare. She rang the bell for Jock, who had cowered out of the room at the very onset of the storm.

'Jock,' she said in a kindly voice, 'is the lock on my bedroom door oiled; does the key turn freely? Good. Oh, and will you tell the maid to make up Mr Mortdecai's bed in his dressing-room, please. And I shan't be down to dinner tonight, I'll just have something on a tray in my bedroom. Thank you, Jock.'

'Oh really, Johanna, now look here ...' I began.

'I prefer not to look there, thank you. I have already

had a hard day. I shall take some light reading to bed with me. Like the airline timetable.'

———·—·—·—·—·—·—·———

It was the cook's night off – it almost always is these days, isn't it? – so when I strolled into the kitchen for a reconnaissance, it was Jock who was setting a tray-load of delicious dinner for Johanna: a nice, thick little *filet mignon* with sauté mushrooms, grilled and stuffed tomatoes and all ringed about with *pommes duchesse* such as I never tire of and side-dishes of *mangetout* peas and Jerusalem artichokes. I rubbed my hands: earth hath not anything to show more fair. 'Give madam *lots* of those carminative artichokes, Jock,' I urged. 'They'll do her a power of good.' He shot me a strange look from his glass eye.

When he returned from the grocery-round, I asked him casually how Madam was.

'Fine, Mr Charlie. Full of beans.'

'And soon,' I murmured spitefully, 'she'll be full of Jerusalem artichokes too, heh heh! But, more to the point, where is my dinner, eh? Or rather, *when*, what?'

'That *was* your dinner, Mr Charlie; Cookie wasn't expecting Madam back today, was she?' The saliva which had been so sweetly flooding my mouth instantly took on all the savour of a panther's armpit. My face, I daresay, grew ashen. Jock was at my side in a twinkling, forcing one of his famous brandy-and-sodas into my nerveless fingers. (The secret of Jock's famous b-and-s's is that he makes them without soda: it is a simple skill, easily learnt.) I swallowed the prescription and pulled myself together.

'Very well, Jock, tell me the worst. Have we to send out for fish and chips or, God forbid, to the Pizza Parlour?'

'Well, I got a couple of gammon steaks ...'

'Hmph.'

'And some of them French mushrooms what I can't pronoun the name of and a few eggs ...'

'Yes? Go on.'

'And I could sortie up some of them Reform potatoes, cooden I?'

'I do not doubt that you could, but all these kickshaws sound more like a light luncheon than a nourishing dinner for a convalescent. Moreover, I am, as you know, eating for two; this moustache will soon contract beri-beri if it does not get its vitamins. Is there nothing to precede this niggardly repast?'

'Yer what?'

'Sorry, Jock. I mean, is there anything for starters?'

'Oh. Ah. Well, I do happen to have a basin of me French pancake batter standing in the fridge but ...' I looked at him levelly. He looked back as levelly as a one-eyed chap can look.

'Oh, very well,' I said and tossed him the key to the cupboard where I keep the caviar. Jock may not be the tastiest evidence of Divine Creation but he yields to none in the matter of making caviar blinis. Nor the making of Pommes Reform, if it comes to that. My fortifying snack was marred only by the compassionate looks Jock cast me from time to time. These looks became even more comp. when he came downstairs from taking Johanna her coffee.

'Madam have anything to say, Jock?' I asked idly as I did a little housework on the moustache.

'Yeah. She asked me if you'd got rid of that excrement yet.'

'Surely she must have said "excrescence"?'

'Oh, yeah, maybe that was the word.'

I picked a pensive tooth.

'Look, Mr Charlie ...'

I raised the toothpick threateningly.

'Jock, if you are going to say "I told you so," pray forget it: the surgeon warned me against flying into passionate rages until I am fully convalescent. If you were going to plead Madam's cause, you may forget that, too. While I have my strength, no-one shall harm a hair of this lip.'

'Matter of fact, I was only going to ask if you'd like a spot of music to sort of put a lid on your dinner,' he retorted in wounded tones.

'Sorry, Jock. Yes, certainly, do wheel on some music, I dote on such sounds.'

Knowing my passion for Grand Opera, what the sturdy

fellow put on the turntable was his treasured 78 mph record of 'Chi mi frena in tal momento' from *Lucia di Lammermoor* – a rather shrewd selection in the circumstances. Now, my own recording of this is sung by Enrico Caruso, Amelita Galli-Curci and three or four other chaps but Jock's rendering is by Shirley Temple and S.Z. 'Cuddles' Zsakal. Jock, you see, has been hopelessly in love with Shirley Temple since the days when he was the youngest delinquent in Hoxton. The record or disc is tuneful, digestive and mildly aperient.

'Thank you, Jock,' I said courteously after he had played it twice. Then I shuffled off to bed, for my wounds still ached in the frosty weather and my moustache needed its beauty-sleep. For a bedtime story I took with me the illustrated edition of Klossowski's French translation of Li-Yu's infamous *Jeou-P'ou-T'ouan*, arguably the greatest pornogram in any language.

My choice of reading was an error, for the *Jeou-P'ou-T'ouan* is not conducive to slumber. Within an hour I was tapping in a tentative, *husbandly* way at Johanna's bedroom door.

'Who's there?' she rasped in unwifely tones. 'I warn you, I am armed!'

'It's Charlie. Your husband, remember? C.S.v.C. Mortdecai?'

'Have you removed that excrement from your face?'

'You mean "excrescence," Johanna, surely?'

'Do I?'

'Oh, *really*. Listen, Mae West has often stated that kissing a man without a moustache is like eating an egg without salt ...' Too late I remembered that Johanna never salts her eggs.

'So go look up Mae West,' she retorted. 'At least you'll have a waistline and age-group in common. There are frequent flights to the US of A; I have just been studying them.' She seemed to be trying to tell me something.

'Oh well, goodnight,' I said.

'Yes,' she said.

I stumbled back to my bed, a broken man.

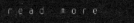
KYRIL BONFIGLIOLI

THE FIVE MORTDECAI NOVELS

'I am Charlie Mordecai. I like art and money and dirty jokes and drink. I am very successful'

Don't Point That Thing at Me

The Hon. Charlie Mortdecai is up to his earlobes in trouble. A Goya painting has gone missing and the authorities seem to think he knows something about it. He does. If he and his thuggish manservant Jock are not very careful, some very nasty men with guns are liable to make them very dead.

After You with the Pistol

It's been made clear to Charlie that he has to marry the beautiful, sex-crazed and very rich Johanna Krampf. The only fly in the ointment is that she seems determined to involve him in her crazy schemes of monarch-assassination and heroin smuggling. Perhaps it's all in a good cause – if only he can live long enough to find out.

Something Nasty in the Woodshed

Charlie has decamped to Jersey after a spot of bother in London, and is hoping to lie low with his manservant and his new bride. But then a friend's wife is attacked, and for once he takes on the role of pursuer rather than pursued.

The Great Mortdecai Moustache Mystery

Charlie's main excitement in Jersey is cultivating an exuberant moustache, even though it endangers conjugal relations. Things perk up when he's invited to Oxford by his old tutor to investigate the cruel and unusual death of a lady don. He uncovers the culprit – but not before coming across enough villains to shoehorn into a stretch limo.

All the Tea in China

After an act of lechery that anyone but a close relative might forgive, Karli Mortdecai Van Cleef, a distant relative of the Hon. Charlie Mortdecai, throws in his lot with an opium clipper bound for China. So begins a staggering adventure. It runs in the family . . .

He just wanted a decent book to read ...

Not too much to ask, is it? It was in 1935 when Allen Lane, Managing Director of Bodley Head Publishers, stood on a platform at Exeter railway station looking for something good to read on his journey back to London. His choice was limited to popular magazines and poor-quality paperbacks – the same choice faced every day by the vast majority of readers, few of whom could afford hardbacks. Lane's disappointment and subsequent anger at the range of books generally available led him to found a company – and change the world.

'We believed in the existence in this country of a vast reading public for intelligent books at a low price, and staked everything on it'
Sir Allen Lane, 1902–1970, founder of Penguin Books

The quality paperback had arrived – and not just in bookshops. Lane was adamant that his Penguins should appear in chain stores and tobacconists, and should cost no more than a packet of cigarettes.

Reading habits (and cigarette prices) have changed since 1935, but Penguin still believes in publishing the best books for everybody to enjoy. We still believe that good design costs no more than bad design, and we still believe that quality books published passionately and responsibly make the world a better place.

So wherever you see the little bird – whether it's on a piece of prize-winning literary fiction or a celebrity autobiography, political tour de force or historical masterpiece, a serial-killer thriller, reference book, world classic or a piece of pure escapism – you can bet that it represents the very best that the genre has to offer.

Whatever you like to read – trust Penguin.